SATAN
HAS SIX
FINGERS

SATAN HAS SIX FINGERS

Vera Kelsey

COACHWHIP PUBLICATIONS
Greenville, Ohio

Satan Has Six Fingers, by Vera Kelsey
© 2023 Coachwhip Publications edition

First published 1943
Audrey Vera Kelsey, 1892-1961
CoachwhipBooks.com

ISBN 1-61646-557-3
ISBN-13 978-1-61646-557-5

1

Her wrist watch marked midnight exactly. Only seven minutes since Jay had telephoned! What had possessed her to seize the first coat her fingers touched and race out of the apartment like a zany? She did not even know where he had been when he called. It might be half an hour or more before he arrived.

Automatically she dipped before the blurred mirror of a peanut-and-chewing-gum machine that bulged from the side of a pillar along the edge of the platform. As she shook her shining shoulder bob into place the mirror reflected an attractive and intelligent face, framed in that soft, dark brown hair. A slender face with clear, candid gray eyes, a short, straight nose, and a mouth whose slender lips were intended to curve up naturally at the corners.

But she saw only that the face was too pale and thin, the eyes shadowed and tight, her lips drooping with fatigue.

"Twenty-seven will seem old enough to Jay without looking haggish," she thought. Fishing a compact from a pocket, she began expertly to work with her lipstick. "I would have had time to glamourize a little—"

She was alone in the vast dimness of the station. At any time a subway station was not an inviting spot, but at midnight how vast and empty and still one could be! And how chill! Above on the streets, the air was cool, too, but alive and sweet after early-June rains. Here all the accumulated mugginess of the long, cold spring seemed concentrated.

She drew her light coat about her and restlessly began to pace up and down. How long till the next train? Five minutes? Ten?

Why couldn't Jay have come to her apartment? Why had he insisted in that low, hurried voice that she meet him in the station? Not only in the station but at the doors of the last car!

Her lips did tilt a little then. Jay was just like his father, Paul Oliver. Paul could generate that same intensity of pressure when he wanted something. Now Jay—and after five years of silence!—had telephoned her to meet him here, and she had responded like a monkey on a stick.

But why such haste tonight if, as he had said, he had been in New York since Wednesday? This was Friday. No, Saturday, really. Where had he been in the meantime that he could not call her? And where had he come from? Not India, surely!

And what would he be like after five years? Her thoughts flew back to that year—that happiest year, perhaps—when, just out of college and the world her own very pearly oyster, she had joined Paul and Eleanor and their adored and adorable Jay in Singapore.

Jay, then a tall, blond giant of eighteen, with steady, laughing blue eyes, had made life a peril for all of them with his outrageous pranks. And a burden for her because of his insatiable interest in everything American. At such times she had found him a little pitiful—so ardently American himself, yet with hardly more than a year of his life altogether spent in his own country.

Suddenly she knew why she had raced out of the apartment and down Seventh Avenue to this stark and lonely station to meet him. There had been neither laughter nor interest in his hurried whispering. There had been fear!

Jay must be alone in New York. And in some sort of jam. Then where were Paul and Eleanor? Still in India? Eleanor's last letter had said something about Universal Electric transferring Paul to another country. . . .

Oh, why didn't she ever answer letters! Then she'd know about her friends. That letter from Eleanor had arrived four years ago! But surely if they had been transferred she would have heard.

She peered into the blackness again. Were those two flecks, like tiny savage eyes gleaming in the depths of the tunnel, moving lights? As she watched, the flecks grew larger, brighter, rapidly. In her ears a faint vibration hummed.

Relieved, she stepped back. What nonsense she had been thinking? She must have read into Jay's words more than he meant. A spring cold could account for his voice. Perhaps all he wanted was a small loan.

Then why was she trembling? The cold, of course. If Jay did not step off this train he would have to come to the apartment. After all, she was a working girl. She couldn't arrive in the office sniffling.

The train was almost on her now. Lights and bumbling roar announced its approach as if it were some celebrated transcontinental streamliner.

Now it was rushing glaring cars past her. Again only here and there a weary passenger sagged against a wicker seat.

As it slowed to a stop she glimpsed two men, chins on chests, hats over their eyes, in the next to the last car. Not far from them an old, fat woman dozed over a basket. A moment more and the train stopped. She found herself within a foot or two of the central doors of the last car.

At first glance it appeared empty. Then as the doors slid back she saw, far down in the corner of a seat, the hunched shoulders of a man, his head bent forward.

That could not be Jay. He would have been standing at the door, waiting to leap out. Disappointed, irritated, too, Penelope turned away. Then resolutely swung back and entered the car. She had to be sure.

Close-cut fair hair beneath the tilted hat, a lean figure in English tweeds, smart topcoat flung about his shoulders, reassured her. Certainly this was Jay.

She tried to keep her voice light, though in the reaction of relief she was angry. "Come out from behind that fedora, Jay Oliver! I know you." When he did not answer she leaned over and pulled up the hat.

Jay! A very tired Jay, she saw then. His face was greenish-white and sunken for so young a man. His eyes were closed. "Wake up, Jay," she urged gently and shook his arm.

Startled, she stepped back, dropping his hat. Jay was moving, but not to rise. He was falling—forward. As she put out an arm to support him he fell against her woodenly, pushing her slight figure back. Then he slumped, a dead weight, to the floor.

"Jay!" She stooped to raise him. Unsuccessful and frightened now, she straightened, looked about. She must get Jay out before they were carried away! How did one hold a train? Why didn't someone come? The pressure of time before the doors closed numbed her power to think.

A warning shudder ran through the train. She abandoned thought of the men in the car ahead. The agent in the change booth—he would know how to hold the train. . . .

As her feet touched the platform a sense of movement behind her spun her round. The doors were sliding together!

She tried to run but could not. Her feet had turned to stone. As the car drew away before her starting eyes her last impression was of Jay's fair head on the grimy floor beneath the glare of light. Then darkness, whirling up in clouds from the concrete platform, rushing in from all sides, sucked her forward and down. . . .

2

"If she wakes in her right mind she may be able to leave within a day or two. For a rest somewhere, of course. But if this fixation about dead men in the subway continues—"

Listening to her nurse's crisp, impersonal voice, Penelope remained with eyes closed, both to hide that she was awake and that she was uneasy to the point of fright. But when Miss Duke's voice faltered oddly she opened one eye. What she saw opened the other.

In the dimness of the corridor, beyond the erect, starched white back a man's forearm, clad in the light wool of a topcoat, had swung up. And the thumb of the doubled hand was jerking an unmistakable invitation for the nurse to join him outside the room. As Penelope watched, Miss Duke stiffened, hesitated, stepped forward, closing the door quietly behind her.

Penelope stiffened, too. Was a closing door always to remind her of those subway doors closing in her face?

She repressed an impulse to ring for the nurse, for anyone, to demand for the hundredth time that something be done to find Jay. Something had been done. With results that had boomeranged against her. That was why her eyes were tight with uneasiness.

Her doctor—Dr. Traine—had listened to her frantic demands. Then after examining her he had given her some little white powders to put her to sleep, and gone his way.

Andrea Mills, with whom she shared an apartment in the Village, had hurried over with flowers and sympathy. She had listened, too, to exclaim, "Poor darling! You must see now you need a long rest." Pepperpot, her editor and friend in need and out, had strolled in with overdone nonchalance. He had assured her the *Chronicle-Leader* could survive if she took a long, long leave. He had listened, also, asked a few questions, and gone away.

But he had returned, armed with books and flowers, possibly in apology for what he had to say. An expert newspaperman, he repeated without implications what he had learned. And he had tipped the scales against her.

No man, ill, injured, or dead, had been found on any west-side, southbound subway train at any hour during Friday night. The agent in the change booth at Houston Street had noticed three or four men, the worse for wear and liquor, stagger off a train sometime after midnight. But when they negotiated the stairs to the street safely he had thought no more about them.

Then, still holding Penelope's gaze with his own, Pepperpot had repeated the words of the unseen man in the change booth of the Christopher Street station.

"She came down here like a bolt out of the blue just at midnight Friday and a train right there if she wanted to take it. But no, she starts pacing up and down like a panther or something. When I don't see her on the next train I run out on the platform. There she was—out cold. Just didn't have the nerve to go through with it, I guess." He had called for an ambulance, and that was that as far as he was concerned.

"And that's that for you, too, Pen, I guess," Pepperpot had concluded. When she didn't answer he had leaned forward to study her anxiously. "Isn't it?"

"I see what you mean," she had admitted finally. "But that isn't that—yet, Pepperpot."

With a sigh he had lifted his long, loose body from the straight bedside chair, fumbled a moment with her pillow, and departed. She had turned to face the white wall and the issue Pepperpot had made so clear without words. She must wake in her right mind—or else!

A dry rustle informed her Miss Dake was again in the room, coming toward the bed. Penelope did not turn or open her eyes. Nor did she move when she thought she felt a cautious hand under her pillow. But the crackle of paper was too realistic a sound to imagine. She turned round and sat up. To see Miss Dake straightening, some letters and a package in her hand.

"What's that, Nurse? Mail?"

Almost human exasperation flicked across the cool hazel eyes. "Did I wake you? Sorry."

With her free hand Miss Dake plumped up Penelope's pillows behind her. "Mr. Murdock—you call him Pepperpot, don't you?—left these under your pillow."

"But why are you taking them away?"

Faint color stained the nurse's untinted cheeks. "I'm not taking them away. That is, I was going to put them on your supper tray—and open this little package for you."

Penelope flushed, too. Embarrassed but troubled by something new and watchful in the nurse's manner, she dropped her eyes. Suddenly stiffened.

Miss Dake's hand, moving toward the pocket of her apron, had jerked away. Penelope's glance, focusing there, spied inside one corner a tiny square of dull green, like mold or mildew. In all her waking hours no blemish had marred those immaculate uniforms and aprons. Certainly that little square had not been there less than half an hour ago when Dr. Traine departed and she had closed her eyes, pretending to sleep. Her idle mind fussed with it irritably. Where in this wilderness of hygienic white could one touch green—much less mildew? Mildewed green . . . She caught her breath. A greenback folded in a tiny square could look like that—through white!

Conscious of the nurse stiffly waiting, she raised her eyes, tried to smile an apology. "I—I guess you startled me, Miss Dake. Don't bother about the mail. I can open it. Andrea brought me scissors in that manicure outfit."

As if in apology, too, Miss Dake gave her scissors and mail, asking idly, "Andrea? Is she with the *Chronicle-Leader,* too?"

"No. Just a friend." Penelope was turning the little square package over curiously, studying its London postmark, the unfamiliar name on the corner card, its various stamps and registered markings.

"You and she live together in an apartment near here, I think she told me?" Miss Dake's words were blurred.

From the corner of an eye Penelope observed the nurse behind her, studying the package also. She dropped it carelessly, face down, on the bed, took up a letter.

"Did some kind friend bring me cigarettes? I could use one now."

Miss Dake moved forward, shaking her head.

"Not even that man at the door when I woke up? Who was he, by the way?"

Miss Dake turned abruptly and started for the door. "Sorry. Just one of the interns asking about Dr. Traine's schedule."

Penelope fixed her eyes on the letter and her ears on the nurse's footsteps in the corridor. When they died away she cut and ripped the package open.

Inside was an envelope, largely inscribed, "Read this first." Beneath it, a carefully wrapped and sealed oval, bedded in cotton. Relief surged over her when she recognized in the agitated scrawl sweeping across the page the boyish tracks of Jay Oliver, only slightly improved.

The first words set her fingers trembling. She gripped the paper tighter to read:

> *Penny—I hope to reach New York before this package. If I do I'll explain and collect it from you unopened when it arrives. If you receive it first, hurry it into the safest bank vault you know. But if you do not hear from me, yet have reason to believe I'm in New York, take it yourself to Rio de Janeiro and give it to Mother. No one else. Cable her through the New York U.E. you are coming. Give any excuse you like, but don't mention me or the package. Open it if necessary for concealment, but don't be too curious about what it contains. And don't think I'm joking! This means everything to many people besides the Olivers. Be careful of it—and of yourself—though if I thought anyone could trace it to you I wouldn't be writing this now.*
>
> *J. O.*

Penelope read and reread the note, each time more slowly and thoughtfully. Her eyes were moist when finally she tore it into bits. How like Jay to say nothing of his own danger! But how unlike Eleanor to permit him to step into any hardship or peril!

Thought of the boy's white face, so drawn and still, sent a tremor over her. If Jay had lost his life attempting to get this to his mother the responsibility he had placed on her was heavy indeed. Swiftly gathering up wrapping paper, box, and bits of letter, she was out of bed, hurrying for her bathroom.

There while water crashed into the tub she unwrapped the little oval. For a long minute she gazed at what she found, incredulous. The longer she looked, the less possible it was to justify either Jay's letter or what she had seen in the subway car.

A crude clay elephant, trunk and legs folded round the body to give it the smooth outline of a very large egg, lay in the cradle of her hand. Surely it was nothing more than another of Jay's amateur efforts at modeling.

When Miss Dake returned with her supper tray Penelope was just emerging from the bath. Her face shone from soap and water. Her long bob was rolled up and bound tightly round her head with a broad green scarf.

The nurse's eyes sped to the bed where letters lay still unopened. "That gift must have been something pretty special to have caused this transformation," she suggested. When Penelope only smiled she added, "I hope it was nothing to eat. Better let us decide your diet for a few days."

Penelope slipped into bed, fanning her wits for an answer. All at once fatigue seemed to have left her. Deep in her heart still lay heavy dread for Jay, but now she knew she had not been deluded, she felt as if her blood had started to circulate again, energy to pour back into her. And now she knew something she could do, she was impatient to do it.

"If that's food," she cried, "give it to me. I'm starving."

Miss Dake arranged the tray on the bed table beside her. Then with a professional glance about the room turned again for the door. "If you don't need me, Miss Paget, I'll take my walk now."

Penelope, deep in thought, ate what was before her with little idea of what it was. A rap on her door brought her upright. When Pepperpot's long head thrust in she sank back with relief.

"Met your private battleship downstairs," he greeted her, dumping more magazines and newspapers on his way to her side. "She said you were all right. That I could come up. But I didn't like that look in your eyes just now. You are all right, aren't you?"

"In my right mind? I've never been out of it, Pepperpot."

He swung the bedside chair around to face her and sat down, smiling. "So—?"

"So—I'm all right. Except—I guess you win. I do need a rest. A long one."

"Any ideas?" He wasn't smiling now.

"I thought of a trip to South America. You know—long sea voyage—tropical sunshine—"

"Rio is a beautiful city, they say. And the Olivers would be glad to see you."

Pepperpot looked innocent "As an editor, Miss Paget, it's my duty to keep up with times. There's a war on, or has that escaped your attention? Many international corporations are bringing their overseas staffs home. I called the foreign department of the Universal Electric to learn their policy on men in foreign service. And, of course, asked about my old friends, the Olivers. Paul, it seems, is now managing director of the U.E. plant in Brazil. Headquarters, Rio."

Penelope could not penetrate behind the righteousness of his gaze. But she knew him too well to believe his words contained only one meaning.

"Then you—you don't think I imagined that telephone call? That I saw Jay?"

He closed one eye slightly. "On that theme, the less said the better. Now I'll as a question. The answer is yes or no. The *Paraguay* is sailing for Rio next Friday night. Do you want me to cable Paul Oliver you'll be on it?"

"Yes." Penelope put out a hand and seized his. "How did you—?"

"I'm asking the questions." He edged his chair forward and dropped his voice. "Have any visitors this afternoon?"

"One."

"Who?"

Penelope looked at him steadily. "I don't know. Miss Dake saw him. Profitably. If she didn't have a greenback in her pocket afterward, my years on your pay roll have been wasted. She said he was an intern—but these little eyes saw what they saw. Why?"

"Andrea. She returned home this evening to find that someone had gone through your apartment with a fine-tooth comb. I've just moved her to a hotel temporarily. And you're to stay right here until that ship sails. Unless"—he edged still closer—"someone else can take it down for you."

Penelope held herself still. "How you talk!" she said lightly after a moment.

"See here, Pen." Pepperpot regarded her sternly. "Whether you've stepped into something deliberately or not, I don't know. But don't try to play this alone. Jay must have been trying to get something to you. That's obvious, isn't it? It is to me—and to perhaps a couple or three other guys who followed him. He didn't have it on him or they wouldn't have searched your apartment. They didn't find it there or they wouldn't have come here to corrupt Miss Dake. They must believe—as I do—that somehow he did get it to you. Perhaps in that package I brought you earlier—"

He sat back suddenly to grin at her. "And, holy mackerel, I know where it is. Very becoming, too. But are you sure you can manage? I'd say Miss Dake's going to earn that money searching your room."

"I'm sure." Penelope's eyes flicked a warning toward the door.

He thrust back his chair and rose as the nurse entered the room. "Friday, then? I'll drive you down myself."

"We win, Miss Dake," Pepperpot informed her. "Miss Paget has agreed to a long rest. If you can hold her together till Friday I'll take her to my mother in Pennsylvania for as long as she'll stay." He looked at Miss Dake gravely. "We consider Miss Paget a very valuable property on the *Chronicle*. If anything upset her we'd take it—very hard."

"How nice! About the rest in the country, I mean." Miss Dake hastily opened the drawer in the table, took out two white packets, poured a glass of water, and stood waiting.

Pepperpot backed toward the door. But there he paused to give Penelope a long glance before he disappeared.

"Till Friday," she said, taking the glass and lifting it to him in salute.

Obediently she opened her mouth for the powders, drank the water, and settled back on her pillows. "Good night, Miss Dake." She closed her eyes lest they betray her knowledge that as soon as the powders held her in sleep the nurse was going to hunt for the contents of that little box.

At that, she thought, those cool hazel eyes might make more out of that little elephant than she could. To her it was just a hard lump, growing harder.

"Four days more," she assured herself, "and Ellie and I will both be at sea. . . ."

Penelope, hidden behind the door of the empty cabin opposite her own, was peering through the slit of the doorjamb.

At that moment the latch of her own door was motionless. But when she had touched it, it had turned slowly, stealthily in her hand.

Someone was in her cabin. Someone intent now on making an unobserved exit. Perhaps he—or she—had felt her hand on the latch. Perhaps had heard some movement when she deserted the door so precipitously.

Her stewardess was off duty at that after-luncheon hour. Her cabin boy, some distance down the main corridor, was sorting a mound of linen. Who, then, could this be?

Crouched behind one door, peering at another as the moments ticked away, Penelope began to prickle with alarm. Could she have imagined that turning latch?

Almost with relief she saw it begin to move again— slowly—noiselessly. Quarter inch by quarter inch her door opened, then swung wide. She stifled the gasp that rose to her lips as for the space of a breath she saw the man who emerged—book in hand! The next he was gone, hurrying down the short passage to the main corridor.

Incredulous, again mistrusting her own senses, Penelope sped for her cabin. Nothing, so far as she could see, had been taken away. Nothing added. Puzzled, she turned to the couch where a mound of *bon voyage* books made a bright spot in the room with their shining new jackets. Seventeen had been given her. Seventeen were there.

Reassured, she returned to her chair in a quiet bay on B Deck.

Only three chairs were set up in that bay. Her own on one side, two on the other. In one, lying as usual with eyes closed and hands quiet on the arms of his chair, was the gentle sad-faced old man she knew only as Dr. Rosario.

In the other, upright, alert, and now annoyed as he caught sight of her, was a small and very dapper young man. Secretary or nurse, he never for a moment left the older man alone. Now his black eyes fixed on her like needles.

Though annoyed herself at his resentment of her presence in that bay, Penelope had no thought for him now. Her attention was for the old man who gave every appearance of having lain in his chair for some time. Yet it had been that old man who had stepped from her cabin! She could not be mistaken.

There was nothing inert or depressed about the secretary-nurse—Senhor Rodrigo, as the old man called him. He guarded Dr. Rosario like an electric eye, aware of everyone and everything that moved on that starboard side of B Deck.

Occasionally he would lean over the older man, talk to him rapidly in some foreign tongue. Sometimes he appeared to plead, sometimes to urge. The last two days he had seemed to command. At first Dr. Rosario had replied in a low, cultivated voice. Since yesterday he had neither answered nor changed expression.

Conscious of Rodrigo's eyes on her now, Penelope half closed her own and settled her head against the pillow. But through her long tilted lashes she continued to watch with increasing interest.

Perhaps because this was the first time she had really concentrated on them, she recognized an antagonism between them. That there was more than sad weariness in the old man's face. That he was not so passive as he looked. His pale lips were set; his veined hands gripped the chair arms until the knuckles stood out in bony ridges, marked with white.

Some change in the insistent voice across the bay roused her. Senhor Rodrigo was standing, his back to her, gesturing furiously as he talked. His urgency contrasted strikingly with the old man's rigid silence.

As she watched Dr. Rosario stirred, opened eyes so deeply sunken beneath bushy gray brows that she only knew from a flicker of the lids he had opened them. Without speaking a word he shook his head in unmistakable finality.

The young man's slender shoulders jerked, sagged. He stood motionless, looking down at his charge as if utterly baffled or defeated. Then with a shrug he turned to the rail to gaze out over the sparkling blue Atlantic. His whole attitude proclaimed his indifference to any further responsibility for his companion.

Fascinated by the intensity of the two, Penelope had not realized how much time had elapsed or that the ship was now humming with activity. Aft on B Deck sailors were rigging a ship's ladder. From A Deck a chorus of voices drifted down, exclaiming, laughing. Turning her glance seaward, she saw the low shores of Barbados slipping by. Pastel-colored houses, green palms, and white sand all blazed with sun.

The beat of the engines changed, slowed, rumbled into silence. The breeze died as the ship swung at anchor. Launches were already speeding toward it. Behind them trailed a fleet of canoes in which Negroes, so brown they appeared purple in the tropical light, shouted and gesticulated as they came.

Although she had no interest in going ashore Penelope did exert herself to reach the rail to watch the Negroes diving into the dark blue depths for coins thrown from the ship. And slowly, while launch after launch filled with shore-bound tourists, she edged aft until she stood near the stairway leading down to the water.

As a launch sped off with the last of the noisy groups an officer raised his arm to wave away the next in line. "No, wait," another said. "Here come two more."

Following his surprised glance, Penelope looked too. Dr. Rosario and Senhor Rodrigo were approaching. Startled by the change apparent in both of them, she stared openly.

The old man came first, slowly, with dignity, but with a heavy, lagging step. His face was set in an expression of

despair, resignation—Penelope could not identify it clearly. As he reached her, his eyes plunged into hers with an
appeal or message so urgent that in instinctive response
she took a step toward him.

Almost imperceptibly he shook his head and passed on
to the stairway. Perhaps Senhor Rodrigo had seen even
that gesture, for his black eyes gleamed with angry suspicion. She turned back to the rail, shaken herself with her
own helplessness to understand or aid.

Again she met the younger man's eyes, for he turned
deliberately on the little platform at the head of the stairway to look back at her. In them she read as clearly as if he
had shouted to her in English a warning that their affairs
were not hers. Then he turned and ran down the steps to
the launch.

Stretched out once more in her deck chair, she could
think of nothing but the old man's face, that deliberate
warning in the secretary's.

3

During the next four days, with the bay on B Deck all her own, Penelope's misgivings vanished. The two empty chairs facing her became merely two empty chairs.

Nothing to trouble her seriously had happened so far. There was, of course, her repeated experience of returning to her cabin to find this or that out of place. But nothing had been taken. And both stewardess and cabin boy had assured her everything she found amiss could have result-ed from the motion of the ship.

Now less than four days remained. But she continued to wear the scarf about her rolled-up bob.

Abruptly the rosy pictures imagination was painting came to an end. Dr. Rosario and Rodrigo were returning to their chairs as if they had never left them!

The voyage, Penelope noted when her surprise at find-ing them still aboard passed, had been working miracles for the old man, too. He appeared younger, stronger. Though he now carried a smart, slender black cane with a heavy gold head, he walked almost jauntily to his chair, dropped into it with an exclamation of satisfaction. Almost imme-diately the eyes beneath the bushy gray brows turned on her with interest and appreciation.

This sea change in Dr. Rosario was not entirely for the better, she thought, amused. What magic could Barbados

possess to have caused it? But the half-smile that curved
her lips vanished when her eyes met those of the secretary. His plunged into hers like strokes of icy steel. If he
had resented her presence before, he was hostile now. And
something else. . . .

She was more disturbed by Dr. Rosario's voice, deeper
and harsher now, and his frequent and throaty laughter.
That is, she was until she saw they disturbed Senhor Rodrigo even more. His role from now on, she observed,
not without satisfaction, was infinitely minor. Dr. Rosario
would do the talking; he, the listening.

Their whole manner of life aboard ship had changed,
she was soon to learn. Until that night at dinner they
had had their meals served in their stateroom. Now they
shared a small table at one side of the dining salon but not
the bottle of wine the old man insisted on ordering for
each meal. Formerly they had always arrived on deck and
left together. Now Dr. Rosario was apt to appear anywhere
at any time, and Senhor Rodrigo seemed incessantly in
pursuit of him.

With little else to occupy her—and because she knew
it enraged the secretary—Penelope watched the metamor-
phosis with curiosity and amusement. Not until the ship
was passing under the nose of Sugar Loaf Mountain into
Guanabara Bay did she understand it.

Passengers crowded the rails to watch the unfolding
panorama of the harbor of Rio de Janeiro. The soft blue
satin waters were dotted with ships and freighters, ferries
and launches, sails of red or white on fishing boats or
pleasure craft. Round the harbor rolled forest-deep mountains with the city of Rio winding in and out and up them.

From the staterooms cabin boys were bringing out hand
luggage to pile in miscellaneous mounds against A-Deck
walls. As a raucous voice rose in anger behind her Penelope
swung round from the rail. A steward apparently had

passed too close to Dr. Rosario. Perhaps jostled him with one of the bags jutting out beneath both arms.

The old man, livid with rage, cane lifted, stood ready to strike. Senhor Rodrigo had jumped in front of him, holding back the raised arm while he motioned the startled and resentful boy away.

"It is nothing, really," a woman's voice near Penelope said. "The voyage has been too long for Dr. Rosario. He is becoming old, like a child."

But Dr. Rosario was not becoming old, like a child! Where had her eyes and wits been? Penelope wondered. The gentle Dr. Rosario she had watched during those first four days of the voyage had had no tones in his low voice to produce these bass bellows. Nor could that frail old man have had either the will or the strength to strike another.

Somewhere two men had changed roles! Where? Barbados? Why? Who was this stranger? And where was the original Dr. Rosario?

Her face alight with understanding and mistrust, Penelope stood motionless, studying the old man, so like, yet so unlike, she saw clearly now, the first Dr. Rosario.

Black eyes thrusting into hers jerked her back to awareness. This time there was more than animosity in Rodrigo's gaze. And she understood, too, what had puzzled her before, his reason for watching her so intently. He had been afraid she would discover the secret of that exchange!

A steward passed along the deck, urging everyone toward the main lounge where immigration and health officials waited to check passports and credentials. Penny turned away with relief. But as she slipped into the line forming outside the lounge she knew that even before she set foot in Brazil she had made a vindictive enemy.

Eagerly as the ship warped nearer and nearer its berth Penny scanned the motley of faces below—white, brown,

black, and every shade between. Nowhere could she find
Paul or Eleanor.

Then her hand flew up, stopped midway, dropped to
her side. Almost directly beneath her a great black cartwheel of a hat had tilted up. For a moment Penelope gazed
down into the dark eyes of Eleanor Oliver.

Penelope pressed toward the gangplank. One of the
first ashore, she stepped into a milling mass of blue-clad
porters, Brazilians, Americans, every nationality, crowd-
ing forward, waving, calling greetings. Clasping her purse
tightly with one hand, keeping a firm grip on her brightly
wound turban with the other, she wriggled and pushed a
way through the mob.

Eleanor's arm went round her, drawing her aside. Eleanor's head bent to kiss her cheek. The wide hat, brushing
her shoulder, hid both their faces. But Eleanor did not
kiss her or offer a word of welcome.

"Have you got it?" she murmured and, when Penelope
nodded: "On you? Here?"

Penelope nodded again. Eleanor stepped back. "Good.
Let's get out of this. Quickly."

Guiding Penelope across the dock to a platform that
ran before what appeared to be miles of warehouses, she
added hurriedly, "I'll tell you later, darling, how thrilled
I am to see you."

Her hand tightened, dropped from Penelope's arm. She
turned to say brightly, "Oh, hello, Cock. Meeting friends,
too?"

Penelope looked up to see a large man whose China-
blue eyes in a broad, smooth, pinkish face flickered with
annoyance. But he answered easily enough, "No. Saw your
car outside and thought Paul might be here." His voice
rose in a question.

"Paul? Leave the Fabrica in midafternoon?" Eleanor
smiled and shook her head. "Sorry, Penny, our secret is

out. This is Mr. Emmett Cochrane, president of the U.E. in Brazil. Cock, this is the Penny you've heard—"

"Penny? Of India? And you wanted to keep her a secret?" The blue eyes beamed on them both, though the beam for Penny was not entirely paternal. "You're just what the doctor ordered, my dear. Pretty young things are rare in these parts—"

"Penny is an exclusive import for the Casa Grande," Eleanor interrupted. "And it's almost four, Cock. We've got to go through customs—"

"Think nothing of it and run along," Mr. Cochrane's expansive gesture dismissed the idea as a trifle. "Our wonder man, Goncalves, is here. He'll see to everything. Just give me your keys, Penny."

As she dug them from her purse and placed them in his hand Penelope was struck again with his impatience at meeting Eleanor there. And Eleanor, too, she knew, though no expression or inflection betrayed it, was on tenterhook to get away.

The keys in his hand, Mr. Cochrane lingered, however, to say, "I must see Paul, Eleanor. Something has just come up. I'll run out later, tell him. And I'll bring Penny's bags with me. If she has a trunk our first truck in the morning can take it out—if that's all right."

"Of course. And thanks awfully, Cock. We'll be on our way then." Eleanor hesitated, added more cordially, "If you're free, why not bring Madge with you and stay for dinner?"

"A big reward for a small favor. We'll be there. *Até logo.*"

Mr. Cochrane hurried away. Eleanor again turned Penelope toward the steps of the platform. At their top Penny lingered to glance back over the colorful dock. Mr. Cochrane, she noticed, appeared in no great haste now. He was strolling toward a high-piled truck.

As she watched two men moved out from its sheltering shade and fell into step behind him with an almost military precision. Dr. Rosario and the secretary!

Silently Penny accompanied Eleanor along the platform into a huge building, through a series of interlocking foyers to a portico overlooking a great square lined with cars and taxis. Stret cars, buses, automobiles, pedestrians flowed in an unbroken stream down one side.

"My car's over here." Eleanor led the way. "Hop in and don't talk until I'm out of this traffic."

She swung the car round the square into the avenue and out of it into a narrower, roughly cobbled street that followed the water front. Penny held her breath as they dodged trucks and cars, finally leaned back and closed her eyes.

What had happened to Eleanor? This cool woman manipulating the car so expertly was almost a stranger. Certainly the little clay elephant had real significance for her. Or had there been bad news about Jay? That steeled expression on Eleanor's usually serene face could only be the result of shock or effort to control some deep emotion.

As the car swerved suddenly Penny looked up to see that they were turning into a wide, short avenue lined with government buildings of some kind. At its head rose a massive gateway, the gates swung wide.

She sat up quickly. "Don't tell me you live behind those imposing—"

"Hardly. Brazilian emperors once lived here. Look back, Penny. Is anyone behind us?"

"Not a soul," Penny reported.

Eleanor swept the car through the gates into an immense park, green and still and empty. Rolling little hills, covered with soft grass, and a meandering stream, all shaded by great spreading trees, formed an oasis after the noisy tumult of the city.

"Good." Eleanor brought the car to a stop on a paved road, her eyes anxious. She glanced at a tiny diamond wrist watch with alarm. "Quick. Where is it, Penny?"

"You want it here?" Penelope looked from Eleanor to the long stretch of deserted green.

"Yes, here. Quickly. I'll explain later. We've only a minute or two now."

In answer Penny unwrapped her turban, shook free her shoulder bob. As it fell, she caught the little elephant wrapped in soft silk.

Eleanor seized it, her anxious eyes lighting. "Darling, how marvelous. In your hair! I've been wretched—thought it was in your purse."

She thrust it under a fold of her skirt between them and sent the car forward swiftly. "Here we go. Keep cool, no matter what happens."

4

As they moved down a dim, tree-arched parkway Penny gazed about apprehensively. Except for a car coming toward them out of a distant tunnel of trees there was not a sign of human—even animal—life anywhere. And Eleanor driving slowly with one hand while she fumbled at her hat with the other, said no more.

Suddenly, though not a breath of air stirred the leaves, the hat swirled out the window almost under the wheels of the approaching car. A moment more and it was tumbling over and over down a grassy bank to a tiny valley.

Eleanor stepped on the brake hastily, brought her car to a stop as the other drew alongside. A chauffeur sprang out, ran round his car and down the bank. An older man descended also, hat in hand and smiling, to step across the intervening space to Eleanor.

"Mrs. Oliver!" His voice was deep and pleasant. "At last the natural laws have caught up with those hats of yours. But do not worry. Guilherme will retrieve this one for you."

His hand entered the window beside Eleanor, took hers, and held it for a moment.

"Dr. Attilio! You won't tell Paul, will you? He loathes that cartwheel." Eleanor laughed and turned to Penny. "This is our good friend, Dr. Attilio de Sousa, director of the glass factory at Fabrica da Luz. And Paul's right hand. Miss Penelope Paget, the missing member of our family, Dr. Attilio." Eleanor's voice was smooth, but to Penny not quite smooth enough.

"Welcome to Rio, Miss Paget." Dr. Attilio's fine dark eyes smiled at her across the wheel, but obviously his mind was not on her. "You arrive at the very best moment— the opening of our winter season. Ah!" He turned as the chauffeur came up with the hat, took it and presented it to Eleanor with a bow. "Here is the flying chapeau."

He held it like a tray, but Eleanor did not take it at once. Penny felt her hand on the seat between them, saw a flash of the little silken bundle as Eleanor's hand moved under the hat and lifted it by the crown. For a moment she held it that way, then quickly tossed it into the back of the car. What became of the little elephant Penelope was not quick enough to see, but she knew from the change in Eleanor it was no longer with them.

Both Eleanor's voice and smile were almost gay with re- lief as she turned again to Dr. Attilio. "You are the second man to do me a kind deed this afternoon. Mr. Cochrane was the first. As a reward I invited him and his wife to dinner. Can I persuade you and Dona Margherita to join us also?'

"You know you have only to suggest, Dona Eleanor. We will be there." Dr. Attilio pressed her hand again, bowed to Penelope, and stepped back.

Penny's eyes admired the tall impressive figure he made against the green. Eleanor, reading her thought, smiled. "He is handsome, isn't he? And truly a *grande senhor.*"

"Well, I must say, Eleanor," Penny retorted, "I never expected you to give that little elephant to the first man we met. You never even looked at it."

Eleanor drove a moment in silence, then stopped the car. "What little elephant, darling? What are you talking about?"

Penelope gasped. "Don't you even know what it was?"

"What what was?" Eleanor's voice was cool and level, too smooth now. She turned and looked Penelope straight in the eyes. "My hat fell off and Dr. Attilio's chauffeur rescued it for me. Is that so remarkable?"

Penny tried unsuccessfully to pierce the enameled smile in Eleanor's eyes. She hesitated, said abruptly, "Perhaps not. But isn't it remarkable for you to dispose of something Jay—Jay and I have had some difficulty getting to you?"

A shadow moved across Eleanor's face.

Her hand on the wheel tightened. "Jay is in Portugal, Penny. Waiting for a plane for Rio."

"Jay is in New York, Eleanor. Or—was. You must know that."

For a moment Eleanor appeared on the verge of becoming the Eleanor of India. Then her face closed and she said crisply, "We'll play it my way, Penny, if you don't mind."

Anger flared in Penelope. "1 think I do mind, Eleanor."

No answer. To Penny's amazement two great tears welled in the brown eyes.

"Eleanor! Darling! What is it? It—it's awful to find you like this—" Penny's own eyes misted.

"I was afraid I'd do that," Eleanor dashed the tears away. "Stop torturing me. Penny. I'm suffering enough."

"Torturing you! Are you completely mad?"

"Sometimes I think I am—or will be. Darling, don't ask questions. Don't mention—Jay. Paul received your cable. Or someone's. It just said you were on the verge of a breakdown, needed a rest—were coming to us." Eleanor gripped Penny's hand, pressed it hard. "Let it be that way, Penny."

She turned away, fighting visibly to regain her composure.

"I—I can't go on," she said more calmly after a moment. "I can't. Penny, if—if I have to think about what

I've done. Talk about it. It's all sealed over inside me. And I've got to keep it that way. Now it's over. My part. Oh, believe me, dear, I did it for Paul—for all of us. But if I— if anything happens to Jay—"

She sent the car leaping ahead and shortly through another great pair of gates out into another busy street. Penelope, flung back in her seat, remained that way, silent, bewildered, increasingly troubled.

From the paved highway they turned into a graveled road, passed a ragged line of small boxlike houses sprawled all over with vivid flowering vines, then turned left. Shortly Eleanor was stopping the car before another pair of gates, closed this time. They sealed solid concrete walls, high but made still higher with rows of barbed wire.

From a white gatehouse just inside a short, dark-skinned man ran out, smiling and bowing, to unlock and swing back the gates. The car shot through, turned left on a paved driveway circling a hill that rose straight from the level ground.

For an instant on the right Penny glimpsed above massed trees the tiled roofs of factory buildings and a soaring chimney. Then on the hilltop above, a long, low house, guarded by three towering royal palms.

Again and sharply Eleanor turned right, sending the car roaring straight up the face of the hill on a white graveled road. Overhead interlaced branches of jack trees formed a dark green vault.

"*A case é sua*—the house is yours, as Brazilians tell their guests." Eleanor smiled. "And it's true for you, Penny. Our house is yours for as long as you'll stay with us, dearest."

Penny glanced at her, startled. Eleanor was smiling as they ran through still another iron gateway, wide open this time at the top of the hill. Smiling as they circled a driveway round the huge rectangular house. Smiling when she stopped the car with a flourish before a wide veranda at the side.

"Here we are, Paul," she announced gaily. "Come, see what I've brought you."

Penny took a moment to look across green lawns, broken by beds of roses and aged, wide-spreading trees to a high green hedge circling everywhere. Then she turned, smiling, too, to see Paul's tall, thin figure running down the veranda steps. The same skinny Paul, she thought affectionately, with the same quick ways, the same big, kindly features and serious steel-gray eyes.

In an instant he was beside the car, kissing his wife, then racing round to draw her out and kiss her soundly, too. She saw then that this was not quite the same Paul. Older in years, yes. That was natural. But older, too, and troubled in spirit. Although he smiled at her she felt he was more anxious than glad to see her.

"This is Penny Paget," he was saying to someone. "Next to Eleanor the passion of my life."

A quiet, brown-haired, brown-eyed man, a little more than medium height, watching from behind the broad railing of the porch, came forward. But Paul, an arm about both Eleanor and Penny, rushed them across the tiled floor into the house.

"Not that it matters," the stranger murmured to Penny as he followed them in, "but I'm Wythe Sloane."

"Matters!" Paul whirled them round. "Penny, this is Dr. Wythe W. Sloane, director of laboratories for Fabrica da Luz—light factory, to you. A very important gentleman, I assure you. Treat him well, for he can poison or blow us all to bits at a moment's notice."

"He only says that to annoy because he knows it eases." Wythe assured Penn amiably. "All he gives me to work with is a little sand occasionally."

"Find some sherry for Penny, dear. And go lightly on that whisky. That is, until later." Eleanor dropped down on a divan and took the glass Wythe had mixed for her. "Cock and Madge are coming for dinner. Oh, and Dr. Attilio and Dona Margherita, too, I think. You'll stay, of course, Wythe?"

Paul, on his way to the dining room, stopped short. Penny saw disappointment flash in his face. Eleanor saw it, too, and smiled at Wythe.

"You'll have to do a good deed to qualify, I'm afraid. There is a sort of reward-of-virtue dinner. Cock rescued us from customs, and Dr. Attilio saved my hat from a sad fate. That is, his chauffeur did."

"My good deed will be to swallow the regrets I was about to offer," Wythe told her. "Delfina likes a balanced table, and I'll make a nice sixth or eighth."

"Why not tenth—if we have to have any of you?" Paul demanded, returning with sherry. "Mart does a good deed hourly on the hour, and his mother is a good deed in herself."

"Ten's too many for Delfina to handle alone," Eleanor protested, "and it's too late to borrow Amelia."

"Ten is not too many, senhora," a flat voice announced from the dining-room doorway. "And Amelia is here."

"See? I told you," Paul declared. "*Mamãe* thinks of everyone else first. She knew you'd need Amelia."

Penny's astonished eyes met suddenly an enormous pair of black ones set in a dark brown face, one of the most sensible faces she had seen in years. It belonged to a short, compact woman in a white uniform, her bare feet thrust into a pair of heelless strapped sandals.

"Delfina's learned to be prepared," Wythe explained to Penny, sitting down beside her. "She's the world's best cook. You'll be lucky to have a meal alone in this house. We flock in from miles around."

"Come in, Delfina," Eleanor invited. "Here is our long-lost Penny. And, Penny, this is Delfina—"

"—our general manager and very good friend," chimed Paul and Wythe in unison, parroting, evidently, some phrase of Eleanor's.

"Miss Penny," the maid said clearly. She looked at the newcomer as if cataloguing her for all time but reserving judgment till later.

"Eight, then, Delfina," Eleanor instructed, rising, and moved toward an arched foyer where a telephone stood on a wall table. "And about eight, too, if you can manage. I'll call Mart to come up and bring his mother for coffee afterward," she added to Paul.

Paul sat still, staring into his glass as he slowly swirled the ice about in it. Then he looked up and smiled at Penny.

"Welcome to Fabrica da Luz, my dear. We've missed you. With Jay in England it's been very quiet here. Too quiet."

5

As she drew an informal dinner dress and accessories from one of the bags the Cochranes brought out with them Penelope registered an impression that Brazilian customs officials were both thorough and untidy. But she was too upset to care.

Why hadn't she had the forethought to ask for a tray in bed? It had been difficult enough to adjust to the new Eleanor, but it was worse to see this new Paul. In India he had had the intense free spirit of the eternally young in mind. Here his high spirits were as false as Eleanor's calm.

She tried to shake off her milling thoughts as she bathed and dressed hurriedly. Perhaps she could have a minute alone with Paul before the others arrived. There had been no opportunity before the Cochranes came, and almost immediately Mr. Cochrane had carried Paul away.

Wythe Sloane had been left in the living room to entertain Madge Cochrane, a small woman so faded and self-conscious that Penny felt sorry for her. She seemed afraid to utter the most casual remark lest it annoy her husband. And Mr. Cochrane seemed to have one ear permanently pinned back for the purpose of suppressing the feeble things she did say.

Or were they feeble? She had asked Eleanor when Jay was expected. And asked Wythe if he still hated living in Brazil. Both questions had been unfortunate. But whether

they were the fruit of curiosity or interest or stemmed
from some deeper purpose, Penny couldn't tell.

Well, Wythe was real enough, though very quiet. He
had the palish look and restrained manner of the indoor
intellectual worker, but he was not unsocial. His pleasant,
courteous manner and easy way of coming to the rescue at
difficult moments must make him quite an asset in mixed
groups. No wonder Eleanor liked him, and Madge Cochrane, too.

In the living room everyone was sipping cocktails,
waiting for her. Dr. Attilio rose cordially to greet her and
to lead her over to meet his wife, Dona Margherita. A tall,
stunning creature, with fine black eyes and gleaming black
hair like her husband's, she was the first woman Penny
had seen who could wear diamonds well. That was fortunate, for they glittered on her ears, fingers, and wrists.
She smiled politely at Penny but said nothing, because,
Dr. Attilio explained, she did not speak English perfectly
so would not speak it at all.

Penny was struck by the change in Dr. Attilio, more so
when she saw that others were noticing him, too. If he had
been a grande senhor that afternoon, he was now a grande
senhor who had just achieved some great victory or triumph. He spoke seldom and with dignity, but some inner
glow radiated from him. Was he under the influence of the
little elephant? She wondered.

When she turned from him she felt other eyes studying
her, looking from her to Dr. Attilio speculatively. Paul's,
Wythe's, Mr. Cochrane's.

Eleanor rose quickly, Madge Cochrane's hand in hers,
to lead the way to the dining room. There she seemed to
solve some detail of procedure by magic.

"We'll place Dona Margherita on Paul's right, Madge,
and Wythe on her right, so they can talk Portuguese. You
sit on my left and Dr. Attilio on my right. That will put

Cock on Paul's left and Penny between him and Dr. Attilio. That way we'll have no shoptalk."

"If I just mention that Mario Soares has returned," Mr.
Cochrane asked when they were seated, "will that be shoptalk?"

"Lord, no!" Paul exclaimed. "Mario's out of the Fabrica for good. Mart's a better superintendent than a dozen
Marios—"

"Good expresses my views in one word," Dr. Attilio
added.

"But not Wythe's," Madge Cochrane's pale blue eyes
were fixed on the chemist.

When Wythe protested it made no difference to him
who was superintendent so long as his laboratories were
not disturbed, Paul laughed and quoted a couplet from
Rupert Brooke:

"And in that Heaven of all their wish, . . .
There shall be no more land, say fish. "

Mr. Cochrane blinked, "I don't get it, Paul."

"Very simple, really," Paul assured him. "Superinten-
dents of grounds measuring in acres and tons and chemists
counting little drops of water, little grains of sand, play
hell with one another."

"At least chemists don't steal lamps," Cock declared.
"Now that we know Mario must have been the ringleader
in that lamp racket we should dig up proof against him
before he disappears again—"

"Why throw good money after bad?" Paul asked. "Mario's out. The thefts have stopped. I'm for taking the loss
and calling it a day."

"And as I told you before dinner, I don't agree," Cock
argued. "If you let Mario go unpunished someone else may
be inspired to steal—"

"I'm inspired to put you both on bread and water," Eleanor interrupted. "One more word about the Fabrica and I will."

"And I'll serve it to them for you with pleasure." Dr. Attilio smiled. "These Americans— To eat, drink, and sleep with their work! That is to shorten life."

"What is the Brazilian way?" asked Penny.

"To consider one's work but a part of life. It has many others—one's home, family, friends, books, amusements, interest—"

"You can say that, Dr. Attilio," Wythe commented lightly, "because work, for you, comes under the head of amusement or interests."

"Before Paul thinks of another poet to quote, I'll second Wythe," Mr. Cochrane broke in. "You Brazilians with a big family fortune behind you can lean back at the end of a day and forget your work. Because you know you can take it or leave it alone. We simple Americans—"

Dr. Attilio's white teeth flashed. "Many of you simple Americans have all you need—and more—but don't know it. What it amounts to really is that you all want more than you have. Not only that, but more than the Joneses have. That is your great vice as a people. At the same time your great virtue—"

The talk rolled smoothly like a well-worn record, and Penny was grateful for it. She could listen politely while she marveled at Dona Margherita's diamonds. Or rather at the fact that she wore them as unconcernedly as an American woman would don costume jewelry.

Remembering the lovely little diamond watch on Eleanor's wrist, Penny looked at Mrs. Cochrane's and found another equally brilliant there. In fact, Dr. Attilio wore a large diamond set deep in a heavy ring. So did Mr. Cochrane. Only Paul, Wythe, and herself lacked a glittering stone somewhere.

She was recalled from her survey of the diamond situation by a growing sense that she was the focus of more than Madge Cochrane's eyes. Paul, she knew, was studying her. She had a physical sensation of the tentacles of his mind trying to enter hers. Wythe's eyes passed over her, returned, appraising, measuring her. And whenever Delfina entered the room Penny felt her great sober eyes. Evidently she met the maid's somewhat stringent demands, for with an ice she received a shy, fleeting smile.

"That makes your welcome unanimous, angel," Eleanor assured her when Delfina had gone. "If Delfina disapproved of you I'm afraid we'd have to send you back on the first boat. She runs us all like good clocks. Even Baroneza. In honor of your arrival she washed the hussy this morning, but she got herself so dirty that she shut her up till tomorrow for her sins."

"Some of those shes have a capital S," Wythe interpreted when Penny looked slightly dizzy. "The capital S. She is a little white dog whose approval you must win also. She's the Baroness in more than name."

"Dear me," Penny sighed. "Life in Rio must be very complicated."

"Not so much so as in New York," Paul told her quickly. "The usual standards of decency are all one needs in Brazil. It's only when foreigners use one standard of good faith among themselves, another with Brazilians, that life can become very complicated indeed."

He smiled at her, then round the table. Penny, startled, saw that no one else smiled with him. Mr. Cochrane's face had flushed pinker still. Eleanor's appeared to have paled under her rouge. Not even Wythe broke the silence. Grasping at the first straw, Penny turned to Dr. Attilio.

"I wish I could speak Portuguese to tell your wife how much I admire her diamonds. I've never seen anything so gorgeous as those bracelets."

Dr. Attilio looked pleased. "I will tell her for you with much pleasure. We are very proud of our Brazilian diamonds."

"Brazilian?"

"But, of course. You do not know that Brazil is one of the leading diamond producers in the world? You do not know of the great Vargas diamond at this moment in New York? From its 726 carats one of the largest jewels in all history could be cut—but won't be. Who could buy it?"

He laughed at her confusion. "Do not be embarrassed. When foreigners think of Brazil they think of coffee. Well, in proportion, diamonds here are as plentiful as coffee beans." He turned to speak to his wife in Portuguese.

For a moment Dona Margherita's eyes rested on Penny austerely then she slipped off her bracelets and passed them across the table. Penny turned them gingerly in her hands, gazing in wonder at their intricate and delicate design. Suddenly, aware that silence was again deep around her, she gave them to Dr. Attilio.

"They are exquisite, but return them to your wife quickly. Before anything happens."

Dr. Attilio spun them on his fingers to catch fire from the candle flames. "You like diamonds? Good. You must let me— Dona Eleanor must take you one day to see our diamond shops."

"And Dr. Attilio must tell you some of his wonder tales about diamonds." Eleanor rose, nodding to Paul. "Let's have coffee around the fire."

"You will be here some time?" Dr. Attilio asked Penny as they moved toward the living room. He skillfully turned her toward two deep chairs some distance from the fireplace.

"Thank you, Dr. Attilio," Penny sighed as she sank into one.

"You sigh? You are very tired? That is why you come to Rio?"

She sat very still, keeping a smile on her lips. Did he think it a coincidence that she and the elephant had arrived on the same day, met him in that park in the same car?

"Good," he was saying. "This is the very place. And time, too. Our winters—ah, they are delightful." He paused as Delfina arrived beside them with tiny cups of Brazilian coffee. "Here you will be able to sun by day and read by that fire at night. You enjoy to read?"

"I've almost forgotten how to read for pleasure."

"Then you will permit my wife and me to place our library at your disposal? We have many English books." His voice dropped. "And you—you did not bring books with you?"

"None of interest to you, I'm afraid, Dr. Attilio. Just light novels, mysteries, the sort of thing friends give as bon voyage presents."

"I may see them—now—tonight?" His voice was lower still.

"Of course. But not tonight. They are coming out in the morning on a truck with my trunk, Mr. Cochrane says."

Across his eyes flashed such concern that Penelope turned her head to see if something were amiss behind her. Only Paul was there, coming toward them with a tray of highballs and liqueurs.

The sound of a car stopping at the veranda interrupted them. Paul gave the tray to Mr. Cochrane and turned for the door, saying, "Remind me to get a butler in the morning."

Obviously the newcomers were a welcome addition. The mother, a short, round little Brazilian woman with a fluff of snow-white hair and another pair of the most enormous and dark, shining eyes. And Mart, a tall, lean, hard-boiled young man with hair like fire. Everyone addressed the mother as mamãe, the son as Mart. If they had other names, Penny did not hear them.

Paul brought the young man to her. "This is Mart, Penny, our superintendent of grounds. Look him over and tell me if he's meant for better things." He patted Mart on the shoulder. "Penny has—or had—an infallible intuition about people." With an odd glance for her he turned to retrieve his tray.

Dr. Attilio rose. "Take my chair, Mart. I have already monopolized the senhorita too long. But save your intuition, Miss Penny. I will give Mart my personal recommendation any day."

Again Mr. Cochrane appeared unexpectedly. "How you Fabrica men stand together! I wish we had the same spirit in the town offices. It's dog eat dog there."

He walked away with Dr. Attilio, and Mart settled leisurely into the chair beside Penny. "And the answer to that," he informed her as he folded, "is that Paul runs the factories. He, the town offices." His long lips twisted cynically. "He'd have us all at one another's throats if he could. Thinks it makes for the competitive spirit. Bigger and better production."

Leaning back in his chair, he surveyed Penny critically. "Not bad. Not bad at all." He lifted his glass to her and smiled. "That's my American blood coming out in me. Want a sample of how my Brazilian side would phrase it?"

"Some other time, if you don't mind. I must do a little homework on the proper responses. Besides, I find no fault with the American way."

"So! Running up the Stars and Stripes on me in the first round! Your intuition must be overrated. I'm a Brazilian and proud of it."

Penny waved her handkerchief feebly. "Peace, brother. I'm just a little stranger in this home."

His hard hand just touched hers, but she felt as if her bones had crumbled. "Americans like our esteemed *presidente* Cochrane get under my skin. I make it a rule to shoot first even when their eyes are a lovely silver gray. Going to be with us long?"

"You can change that record, too." Penny sat up, feeling sprightly for the first time since she arrived. "Everyone asks me that. What's the matter? Don't you welcome little strangers?"

"Speaking for myself no. Especially young femmes. Too much fag combing them out of the hairs."

She looked pointedly at his blazing thatch. "Dead or alive?"

His shouts of laughter startled the room. Dona Margherita's eyes smoldered with distaste. His mother shook her head at him, but the others waited expectantly.

Mart waved a nonchalant hand. "Purely local humor." Then he looked about the room anxiously. "Did we miss anything by not being invited to dinner?"

"Mart!" His mother smiled an apology at Penny. "The poor boy thinks he's giving an imitation of an American—"

An unexpected voice answered Mart. "Penny introduced a new topic," Madge Cochrane said. "Diamonds."

Penny looked about the suddenly silent room in astonishment. Only Eleanor retained the power to move and speak. Her eyes on the toe of a gently swaying slipper, she suggested, "Tell one of your diamond tales now, Dr. Attilio. A dark and chilly night, friends about a fire—the perfect setting."

A feeling of helpless resentment touched Penelope. That meeting with Dr. Attilio in the park was no accident. Perhaps this dinner hadn't been as impromptu as it appeared, either. And now she felt she was being used again to further some purpose or previous arrangement of Eleanor's.

But Dr. Attilio was taking it all very naturally, making the usual courteous deprecations. "Miss Penny has given me the perfect opportunity," he admitted finally, "to tell you a story I want you all to know."

6

"The beginning," he said, "dates back fifty years before my family entered the story a century ago. At that time diamonds were pouring out of the mines of central Brazil in what appeared to be an inexhaustible stream. No accurate figures exist as to their quantity, but it is known that during one period of less than thirty years more than a million and a half stones were mined. And shipped across the seas to Portugal. Every stone had to be sent to Lisbon and every stone of twenty or more carats automatically became the property of the King.

"Naturally that resulted in a great deal of contraband—what you call bootlegging in the States. Miners who found particularly fine or large diamonds frequently hid them, hoping to retrieve them later when conditions might have changed. Penalties for hoarding and bootlegging were very severe. Guilty miners, if caught, were exiled to Africa and all they owned confiscated.

"One day—about 1796—two simple miners named João and José, and that's almost all that is known of them, found a stone so large they could not believe it was a diamond. But if it were, they had no intention of letting it fall into the hands of others. Yet neither trusted the other to guard it. So they made a pact to remain together day and night. Each one, I believe—though this is pure legend—was to possess the stone on alternate days. At any rate, their inseparability raised suspicion. One morning both were found dead. Murdered."

Dr. Attilio turned to look at Penelope.

"Don't stop," she urged. "If it continues like that you should sell your story to Hollywood."

"It does continue like that," he assured her gravely. "The man who stole their diamond was a Portuguese named Antonio. He belonged to the Regiment of King's Dragoons stationed in the mines to maintain order and to spy. Antonio also could not believe a diamond could be so large. He made the mistake of asking someone's opinion. He, too, was found dead. And so the stone went from hand to hand until whenever a man was found mysteriously murdered it was whispered that the great diamond had been in his hands.

"The stone even acquired a name—Satan's Sixth Finger. There is a superstition among the simple people of my country—of many countries—that the devil has six fingers. Anyone unfortunate enough to be born with six fingers is considered to be in league with the devil and doomed to lead a most unhappy life. Today modern medicine saves many victims by removing the extra digit when the child is born. But in remote regions owners of six fingers are still suspected of being Satan's emissaries.

"Sometimes Satan's Sixth Finger would disappear from sight for a year or more. Then the discovery of another murder victim would revive the rumor that the stone was again in circulation. Finally the fact of its existence became generally accepted, though no one would credit the tales told of it, for it was said to be as long and wide as a hen's egg and more than half as thick. Incredible!"

Dr. Attilio paused to sip his drink. No one spoke. His glance went round the room to Paul and, still looking at Paul, he took up the story again:

"One hundred years ago this house in which we are sitting tonight had already for many years been the Casa Grande of my great-great-grandfather's fazenda here. To-day Dona Eleanor's skill has made it a *placete* of only six or seven rooms. But in those times, Brazilian families being notably large, it included twenty or more small ones.

"My great-great—he was the Barão de Avila—to be brief, I'll call him Baron. A very rich and powerful man, and a hidalgo of the empire of Brazil, as those remaining royal palms beside the Casa gates testify, he had twelve children, three of them sons. Of the three, the oldest was his only child by his first wife, a beautiful young woman he had loved passionately. Everything he had, everything he did, he had and did for the sake of that oldest son. Romerão. This gave no pleasure, it may be imagined, to his remaining sons nor to their mother.

"Romerão was proud—as all my family are. And adventurous—as many of us today are not." Dr. Attilio smiled deprecatingly and turned his eyes from Paul.

"Sometimes the young man would disappear for weeks, but he always returned. And sometimes the information he brought his father was extremely useful—either for Baron Avila's economic interests or for his political role at court.

"One night the baron had a dream which caused him to leap from his bed. In it he had heard the voice of Romerão calling him. Romerão had been away longer than usual, and Baron Avila was tremendously worried for his safety. So now he roused the house and sent his other sons with slaves to look for him. And in a passion of anxiety himself, he set off down the back of this hill toward a road that used to run through a small but deep ravine.

"That ravine was filled and level when the U.E. bought this property. The glass and lamp factories stand on it now. But a century ago it was deep and narrow and dark.

In it the baron found Romerão. The young man was dying. He had been stabbed in the back."

Someone sighed. Someone jerked a chair. But no one turned his gaze from Dr. Attilio's strained and intent face.

"Baron Avila called no one, not even a priest. He remained through the night beside his son until the boy was dead. Then he carried Romerão up the hill in his own arms to this house. After Romerão was buried the baron shut himself up in a room for days, hardly eating or sleeping. When at last he appeared he seemed on the verge of death himself.

"But he did not die—then. On the first ship to leave Rio he sailed for Europe. He was gone some time. No one knew why he went or where or what he did abroad. No one ever knew so long as he lived." Dr. Attilio paused and smiled round the silent circle. "That is the end of the beginning."

"There is more?" Wythe Sloane asked.

"Of course." Dr. Attilio glanced at his wife. "But perhaps I have already talked too long—"

"No point in cutting off a dog's tail by inches," Mart drawled. He grinned at Penny. "Inherited that pretty thought from my Texas father."

Slowly, carefully, as if choosing each word, Dr. Attilio went on.

"About a year ago I received a letter from the Bank of England in London. It enclosed a sealed letter written by Baron Avila just a century ago. I'll spare you details of how it came to me except to say that I am a direct descendant of the son born to Romerão's young wife after his death. That letter told me the story I have just told you. And it told me much more. It told me the baron had received from Romerão in that dark ravine Satan's Sixth Finger."

Again that sigh. Some movement. But Penny could not turn her fascinated eyes from Dr. Attilio's face to see.

"In that letter Baron Avila also told of his intention to end the evil of the diamond by hiding it away for a century. And he told where the stone was and how to get it."

A tremor of cold ran over Penny. Her eyes felt stiff from gazing at Dr. Attilio. Around her some stifling emotion seemed to be rising from the room. Why didn't someone speak? Break the tension?

Again Mart came to the rescue. "You found it?"

Dr. Attilio raised a hand dramatically. "The date to find it is still to come."

Tautness went out of Penny as relief poured over her. How ridiculous to have supposed that silly little clay elephant could have concealed the great stone—that for almost three weeks she had sheltered in her own hair Satan's Sixth Finger.

She looked up to find Dr. Attilio watching her anxiously. "You do not enjoy such tales? When you are so very tired I was unwise to begin so long a story—"

"Unwise to tell it at all, in my opinion," Mr. Cochrane declared. "Do you realize what a plague your life will be, Dr. Attilio, if this story gets about? Why, you might even be in danger someone—"

"—might try to kill me for the information?" the Brazilian finished for him. "Someone who desired the diamond for himself?"

"Well, something like that," Mr. Cochrane was embarrassed. He looked around, "I suggest that each of us here solemnly promise not to repeat or write or in any way communicate to anyone else this fascinating but very dangerous story of Dr. Attilio's."

"But I want you to repeat it," Dr. Attilio protested. "That is why I am telling it. I want you to repeat it as often as you like. When I have finished telling it all, of course."

"There is more?" Penny cried. "Oh, don't spoil it, Dr. Attilio. It's perfect as it is."

"I must tell it. Fortunately the end is brief. Perhaps Baron Avila left other letters with the Bank of England. I do not know. But someone somewhere knows something of this tale. Perhaps talked unwisely. I have just received word that a kinsman of mine is—is mysteriously dead—in Barbados."

Barbados! That name clanged in Penny's ears. She hardly heard Dr. Attilio's next words.

"Perhaps he paid with his life for the folly of talking too much. Too soon. A terrible folly—for others may make the same mistake—may swallow the tale whole. As I did, at first."

"It isn't true?" Paul asked that. He was sitting beside his wife on the divan, his hand through her arm, closed about her wrist, hard. Eleanor leaned back against the couch, her eyes half closed, her face rigidly calm.

"The tale as a tale is authentic, yes. But the diamond may not exist."

Dr. Attilio sat back, pleased at the effect of his statement. "Wait! Wait! Let me finish."

The rustling and talk ceased.

"I investigated. I wanted to know two things beyond all doubt. First, if such a diamond really existed. More importantly, if it had been given to Baron Avila by his dying son Romerão."

"And you found?" Wythe Sloane prompted.

"That if such a stone exists at all it never became the property of anyone in my family."

"How could you prove something like that which happened a century ago?" Mr. Cochrane demanded.

"The task was not too difficult. The women—some of the men, too—of my family have been faithful diary keepers. Family historians, we call them. And according to old diaries of the time of Romerão, his death was due to the very natural cause of having roused the jealousy of a lover for his lady. No one, but several diaries record that.

"They also record that the baron, brooding over the death of his oldest son day after day, without food or sleep, became from that time on the victim of hallucinations. He knew—as did everyone else—the old legend that death followed Satan's Sixth Finger from hand to hand. What more natural then that he should prefer to link the death of his best-loved son with a fabulous jewel rather than with a sordid affair over someone's mistress? Remember, we are a proud family."

"But that is merely assumption on your part," Mr. Cochrane protested, added hastily, "About the cause of Romerão's death, I mean."

"Wait. The instructions in the letter Baron Avila left to be delivered to the head of the family when the century had passed obviously reveal the invention of a deluded mind. You will have to take my word for that. But finally I must confess this: Crazed over the death of Romerão, Baron Avila took his own life. Shortly after he returned from Europe. That is an act the law of our church forbids. To a man of such piety as my ancestor, it would not have been possible had he been of sound mind."

Dr. Attilio rose, smiling apologetically. "I have taken too long with my story, and my wife is chiding me with her eyes. But you can understand why I am eager for you to tell it if the lives of innocent men are not to be endangered. I am sure you agree with me now, Mr. Cochrane?"

"I? Oh yes, yes indeed," Mr. Cochrane rose stiffly. "I should have waited until you finished your tale before offering advice." His voice was dry as he said good night to Dr. Attilio. Then, "Come Madge," he urged. "It's late. Can we take you in, Wythe?"

"Thanks. My car is waiting for me beside the laboratories." Wythe rose but made no move to go.

The Cochranes hurried away, and Mart's mother prepared to follow.

"How do you like the Rio brand of bedtime story?" Mart asked Penny as he waited for his mother. "Whew! With that deep voice of his, the doc had even my hair on end for a time!"

"Depends on how much of the yarn is true," Wythe said idly. "Come on, folks. Can't you see the Olivers are dying to be alone at last with Penny?"

"How much is true?" Eleanor repeated. "Why not all of it?"

Wythe smiled. "My nose was in exceptional form tonight. If I ever smelled a herring that tale was one. But which was herring and whose trail it was meant to cross—" He shrugged. "Well, *até logo*. Don't let them keep you talking all night. Penny."

The smile vanished from Paul's tired face as he closed the door behind them. He walked straight to Penny and, lifting her out of her chair, demanded, "Now, then! What about Jay?"

Behind them a tray of glasses clattered in Eleanor's hand. "What about Jay, Paul? I told you Jay is—"

Paul did not turn his harassed eyes from Penny. "Believe Jay is in Europe if you wish, Eleanor. I know better. I knew something was on our Penny's mind when she did not leap out of the car to meet me. And I watched her eyes when I said Jay was in England. What happened, Penny? Where is Jay?"

Penelope stood miserably in his tight grasp, then admitted uncertainly, "He was in New York, Paul. I talked with him on the phone, saw him for a moment. But I don't know where he is now—"

Paul placed her back in her chair. "Now begin! Tell me everything you know."

For an hour he questioned her, going over and over her experience that Friday midnight in New York.

"But nothing's happened to Jay; can't you see that?" Eleanor insisted at intervals. "Penny wasn't herself that night. If Jay is in New York and she did see him in the subway—that doesn't mean he's ill now or—"

"Dead?" Paul's voice was bleak.

"He isn't dead! Don't say that. We—we would have heard. The New York offices—"

Paul rose to pace the floor. "He may have known he was followed for some reason." He did not look at his wife. "He may have faked a faint to keep Penny out of trouble. He could have left the train at the next station."

"I'm sure that's what he did if—if it were really Jay she saw," Eleanor agreed. "He would not have been able to reach her again that night, remember?"

"You're sure he made no effort to see you again?" Paul interrupted. "Think, Penny. You did not go back to your apartment. He could not reach you there or the *Chronicle*. But wasn't there anything in the papers? Couldn't he have learned you were in a hospital?"

Penelope stopped a shake of her head midway. "Some man did come to St. Simon's. It might have been Jay."

"Of course, it was Jay," Eleanor declared impatiently. "When he learned what had happened to you he would have been worried to death. How could he know when he telephoned you were on the verge of a breakdown?"

"Wait, Eleanor. What makes you think this man wasn't Jay, Penny?"

"I don't know. Something about the gesture this man made. I—I just saw his hand, really. And he gave my nurse money—I'm sure of that—to watch me and my mail. That didn't seem like Jay."

Eleanor laughed brittlely. "To buy you books or flowers, silly. He was probably so ashamed of himself for placing you there, he didn't want to face you." She rose. "Oh, go to bed, both of you. You're making a mountain out of a molehill."

"You could be right, Eleanor," Paul admitted. "But none of this explains why we haven't heard from Jay. Why didn't he take a plane down or come on the *Paraguay* with Penny?" He started to pace the floor again.

"Paul!" Eleanor stopped him, her hands on his shoulders, forcing him to look at her. "Don't—don't say any more. I—I didn't know you knew—where he was. I can't bear it, Paul. You think I sacrificed our son for—"

"For—"

"For a chance to have a home in our own country. For Jay and for you and me, Paul. You know how much he wants it. I do, too. He is an American boy. He wants American friends, American life. It's been so long, dear, and he's had so little of it. Every year you say, 'Two more years and we'll go home.' And we believed you and waited. But now we don't any more. You said it in Japan, and you said it in India, and now you're saying it here. But you know and we know that the moment you've finished this plant you want to go on to the Argentine—"

"So you took this way to—to get money—for a home!" Paul's hands flashed up to close on hers and hold them tightly. "I didn't know you both wanted it—so much."

"And I couldn't know there was such danger, Paul. Jay is so intelligent and resourceful. And Cock—"

"Cock!" Paul released her, stepped back. "What about Cock?"

"He—he just made the arrangements for Jay to fly to Portugal and go on to London and back. Cock doesn't know why, Paul. He did it because I asked him."

"Someone knows. Someone talked. One man is dead in Barbados. And Jay—my son—"

Penny slipped away. Slipped away with an awful knowledge that Dr. Attilio's tale was true!

Jay must have gone to London to secure Satan's Sixth Finger for Dr. Attilio. Unable to return to Rio with it, he had sent it to her, then followed it to New York.

And she had brought it to Eleanor in that horrible little elephant. . . .

7

A warm and breathing weight on her stomach woke Penny. She blinked at sight of an enormous and spotless powder puff sitting upright to regard her with two bright eyes of its own.

"How do you do?" she asked.

A snowy paw came up, inviting itself to be shaken. Penelope shook it solemnly. The next moment she became a hillock over which the puff raced back and forth, emitting incessant, earsplitting barks.

"How do you do?" She tried again.

The fluff sat down and offered a snowy paw.

Many times in the days to come Penelope was to wish she could still the mystery and horror tightening around her with a "how-do-you-do." But at that moment she only knew she had fallen captive to the most ingratiating and tyrannical little dog in the world.

Suddenly the Baroneza dropped down beside her and closed her eyes in what appeared to be deep and prolonged sleep. Looking around, Penny found Delfina standing in the doorway.

"Good morning," she cried. "Or is it morning?"

Delfina came slowly into the room, her face so dark and somber that Penelope sat up to look at her more closely.

"It's almost three, Miss Penny."

For the first time Penny became aware of the brilliant afternoon sunshine flooding her room and of the silence in all the home.

"Oh, why didn't someone wake me? And where is every-one?"

The maid's eyes shone unexpectedly with tears. "They're gone, Miss Penny. This morning." Fumbling in her pocket blindly, she drew out a letter. As Penny ripped it open Delfina picked up the Baroness and turned for the door. "I'll get you something to eat."

But she didn't move. Holding the wriggling Baroneza tightly, she watched Penny's eyes widen.

You must understand and forgive us, darling. Paul and I are taking the five-o'clock plane for New York. There was nothing you could do, so we didn't wake you. You're to stay right here and rest and sun and be well when we return. Delfina will see to that. And if you want amusement or advice or anything, go to Wythe Sloane. I'm leaving him a note to keep an eye on you. Heaps of thanks for coming, and don't worry. I know Jay is all right. But Paul insists on going, and, of course, I can't let him go alone. Heaps of love, too, angel. We'll be back the first possible moment—all three of us. Eleanor.

And across the bottom of the page Paul had scrawled:

Sorry, Penny, but you know how I feel about Jay. Take it easy here and don't worry about us. The house is yours. If you get into mischief go to Mart. Till soon, my dear, P.

Penny dropped the letter to find Delfina waiting beside her.

"Oh, why didn't they wake me? What time did they go?"

"There was no time, Miss Penny. The plane left at daylight, and they had to go into Rio as soon as they could. They did not know if they could get places on the regular plane. But Mr. Paul said he would get a special one. He telephoned just before five o'clock that they could go."

Penny threw back the covers and swung her feet to the floor. "I'm getting up, Delfina. How about some food on the veranda?"

To shake off the depression settling over her she sped to shower and dress in gray flannel slacks and shirt. At sight of them Delfina, sadly arranging a tray in the kitchen, lifted startled eyes.

"Don't worry," Penny assured her, misunderstanding. "Mrs. Oliver promised they would soon be back."

Delfina moistened her lips. "It's about Mr. Jay, isn't it? If he is in Portugal why do they go to New York? You bring bad news, Miss Penny?"

Penelope shook her head. "I guess you and I will just have to hold the fort until they return and tell us."

Delfina picked up Penny's tray and led the way to the veranda. And without a word Penny followed her. But when she was seated Delfina did not leave. Something else obviously weighed on her mind. "You brought something with you, Miss Penny?"

Penelope put down her melon spoon carefully. What now?

"Your trunk and books came out this morning. I unpacked them while you sleep. Your trunk, I mean. The books are on top of the wardrobe in your bathroom if you want them. But, Miss Penny, everything is tumbled and messy. Not like the senhora's trunks when she comes home. The customs must think you brought something—"

Penny's thoughts raced back to her tumbled bags of the night before. "Nonsense," she said with more assurance than she felt. "Friends packed for me and very quickly. I was sick, you know. And baggagemen simply throw trunks and bags around."

Halfheartedly she followed the whisking little dog about, stopping to glimpse in the distance everywhere blue mountains against a clear indigo sky.

The Casa Grande was truly a big house, she realized as they circled it, and colorful with its roof of crimson-toned tiles and sprays of crimson bougainvillea against creamy stucco walls. And roses, dahlias, and zinnias amazing in size and height. Even violets, tucked away in the shade of the low building at the back that housed garage, laundries, and servants quarters, were three times the size of any she had ever seen before.

A fattish, slow-moving gardener clipping the hedge stopped to smile at her and to laugh at the Baroneza's stubborn efforts to find a point to wriggle through—though gates front and rear were wide open. Brushing aside some dry-rustling dark leaves, Penny saw in the intricately interlaced and ironlike branches that the little dog was as helpless as before a concrete wall.

Temporarily convinced herself, the Baroneza led Penny to the tall Casa gates. Penny caught her breath as she looked beyond the Fabrica walls to a wide green valley ruffled with little hills and, farther still, to the crests of the Organ Mountains. Above her soared the three royal palms, their restless fronds brushing the sky. But their noble grace reminded her of Dr. Attilio and his story, and she turned from them quickly to explore with her eyes the forbidden land beyond the gates.

To the right of the driveway an old orange-and-grapefruit orchard covered the slope. To the left spread vegetable gardens, so extensive they were evidently the source of supply of the Fabrica's restaurants.

The U.E. plant, she discovered, could only be seen from the rear gates, from which another road led down a more gradually graded slope to wide green lawns. Beyond them the red tiled roofs of factories, warehouses, and other buildings spread about the foot of the hill.

Delfina came to shepherd Penny and the Baroneza round the house to the veranda. The maid hesitated, then asked: "Will it be all right if I go to my sister's? When the senhora does not need me I go see her."

"Of course. If no one comes. I can't speak Portuguese, you know."

"I will come back by eight and you will be all right here. The gardener and chauffeur are gone now. By six everyone will go except the watchmen at the north gate and two firemen that stay in the glass factory all the night."

"The north gate? Is that the main entrance—where the gatehouse is?"

"The only one. And no one can come in there, even the workers, without a card of *identidade*. Everyone else must wait till the gateman telephones for permission to let them in. No one will come up here, Miss Penny."

Her voice came to Penelope from far away. Sleep was claiming her again.

When she opened her eyes Delfina was still beside her, still talking. But the sky was deepening to black, and darkness clung about the veranda.

"Wake up, Miss Penny. See, you have slept four hours and will be cold. I was afraid when I came back and saw the Casa dark."

"I'll take the Baroneza for a walk. It's all right to go now, isn't it?"

Delfina looked at her for the first time with approval.
"Then senhora always walks an hour about the pavement
when she is home. But you cannot stay out that long, Miss
Penny. The clouds are heavy. Rain is coming soon. What
are you looking for?"

"The Baroness." Penny turned at some startled sound.
"What's the matter?"

"The Baroneza was shut up in my room, Miss Penny.
I—I heard her there when I came in. I fed her, and she is
sleeping there now."

"Shut up in your room?"

Delfina nodded, her eyes intent. "She did not bother
you? You did not put her there?"

"Of course not. I was asleep before you left the veranda." Penelope turned uneasily toward the doors. "Do you
think we—we'd better look in the house? That someone
has been here?"

Delfina laughed unexpectedly. "Mr. Mart! That's who
it was. I saw him running down the back road to his shops
when I came. He must have come up here and the Baroneza tried to follow him. *Pobrezinha!* She is lonely for the
senhora."

Penny said hastily, "If it's going to rain I'd better start.
I'll get a jacket."

Delfina followed her inside, turning on lights, closing window draperies, finally accompanied her to the rear
gates with final instructions.

"I will lock these gates now, Miss Penny. Will you come
up the driveway and through the Casa gates? You have only
to pull up little blocks at the bottom, and shut them hard.
They lock themselves. Good night, and don't be afraid if
you hear a whistle in the night. It is only a watchman. One
goes round outside the hedge every hour."

Smiling to herself, Penny set off down the back road
to the brightly lighted pavement that ran round the hill.

Delfina was definitely taking her in charge. And more than the Baroneza was lonely for the senhora. All that about locked gates and watchmen sounded as if Delfina were whistling to keep her courage up. Wasted breath, she thought, amused. Mart evidently had the situation well in hand!

When she reached the pavement and saw the high wall, its top glistening with broken glass in addition to the tiers of barbed wire, her sense of superiority over Delfina increased.

"The place is a fortress. If only Andrea and Pepperpot could view me now. Miles of private park to walk in while they, poor city sparrows, are lucky to see a tree."

For an hour she rambled back and forth on the pavement, enjoying the cool night air, the crowded stars in one section of the sky while all the rest was ebony black, the exotic patterns thrown by swaying branches of flamboyant and mango trees on the concrete and against the cream walls of the buildings.

When at last she approached the north gate on her way round to the Casa driveway the gateman came out of the gatehouse to smile a *boa noite*. Then he pointed to the sky, turned up the collar of his dark cape, and hurried back a few steps. Taking the hint, she started at a brisker pace for the Casa.

Not until she left the pavement for the tunnel of the jack trees did she realize how dark the night had become and how close the rain. Before she had climbed many feet the first drops were pushing through the thick leaves to plop on the gravel.

Once or twice she paused, breathless with the climb, to feel them on her flushed face. Then as the rain fell more heavily she stopped no more.

Her heart was pounding with the exertion, her knees trembling when she reached the Casa gates. One already was closed. Shielding her face and holding the collar of her jacket together with her left hand, she stooped to release the bolt at the base of the other with her right.

Her hand never touched the gate or found the bolt. Her fingers remained rigid in mid-air where some nervous reaction had jerked them.

The drumming of the rain fell round her unnoticed. What she had heard, clearly and unmistakably, was the crackle of the hedge as something thrust against it sharply. What she felt was a cold chill of menace as tangible as the rain in the air.

She knew that crackle. Only a few hours before she had heard it over and over as the Baroneza tried to push a way through the twined and heavily leaved branches.

The Baroneza certainly was not outside those Casa gates in this rain. But something or someone was certainly standing or moving along the hedge on the low bank just above her! What, she did not wait to learn.

Reaching the house was like running over quicksand in a nightmare. Her feet slipped on the wet gravel, slipped on the wet grass as she ran across it to the front door, remembered it was locked, and swerved round to the side veranda.

Light shining through the draperies gave her courage. She raced up the steps—to fall headlong on the cold smooth tiles!

For the space of a breath she lay motionless while her heart tried to tear itself loose from her breast. For the first time in her life she knew terror. A heart-choking, breath-stopping terror. Then she sprang to her feet and whirled round.

Something darker than the darkness sprawled across that upper step. And across her terrified mind flashed again the sensation her hand had known as she fell. Of something sharp. Of something warm and stickily wet. Of some heavy, unresponsive softish mass.

She tore her eyes from that dark shape and fled for the doors. But she could not rip from her mind the knowledge that what she had touched was the lifeless body of a man.

He had slipped and struck his head on the hard tiles, she tried to tell herself as she fumbled at the doors, was unconscious, needed help. But once inside, memory of that rough and jagged bone that had pierced her hand, now stained with streaks of red, told her he was dead.

Doors locked and bolted behind her, she knew she was safe from whatever horror lurked outside. They were almost impregnable. The windows were decoratively but no less effectively barred and, in addition, screened.

They could not, however, shut out the terror that had come in with her. Nor her abysmal feeling of helplessness as she sped across the bright living room to the kitchen to scrub frantically at her hand.

She could think of no one to whom to turn for help. Delfina might be a tower of strength by day, but she was emotional and superstitious. If waked now to learn that a dead man lay on the Casa steps she might walk out, have hysterics, or both.

Wythe Sloane lived somewhere in Rio, ten or fifteen miles away at least. Mart? He and his mother lived near the factory, but she had no idea where, nor even what their surname was to call them. The Cochranes lived near Wythe, somewhere on a mountain.

She had no Portuguese to call the gatehouse of the police. And neither course seemed wise. The night gateman might be capable of handling the gate competently, but that, she feared, was the only egg in his basket. Certainly, either for her own sake or Paul's, it would be a mistake to become involved with the Brazilian police.

With relief she remembered the night watchmen. One of them circled the hedge every hour, Delfina had said. Perhaps she thought wildly, a watchman was responsible for that man on the steps. Perhaps he had seen an intruder entering the Casa gates, struck him down, and gone for help.

Somehow she pushed herself out of the living room, through the foyer, into a reception hall with the proportions of Grand Central Station. And across it to the massive front door. From there she could watch the Casa gates, attract the watchman's attention. . . .

Propping her five feet three inches against it, she peered out through a high, small pane. All she could see was rain driving through darkness.

Her fingers found switches in a row just inside the door. While she peered she pushed down quickly one key after the other.

Porch lights and garden lights and gate lights flooded on, revealing lawns and rosebeds and trunks of the royal palms. Revealing, too, that one half of the gate was still closed—that the other half was slowly closing.

Some hand, invisible to her, must have released the bolt and thrust the gate forward. Must have released it but an instant before she pressed down the switches.

The watchman! But before the thought was finished she knew it was not the watchman. Blurred by the rain though still penetrating, his whistle sounded. It was coming up the back road to the rear gates.

For a moment her body went limp against the door, then stiffened. That sharp rustle of the hedge again crackled like thunder in her ears. Something—no, someone!—had stood there above her—frightened her—frightened her deliberately so that she would not close the gate.

Cold with a thought—an explanation—for that rustle, she turned round. A moment later she was in the living room, a reluctant finger hovering over the inside switch that controlled the veranda lights.

Decisively she pressed it and, slipping aside the drapery of a window, looked across the veranda to the steps.

She saw nothing but red tiles shining with moisture and rain falling in a heavy cleansing torrent.

8

When Penelope arrived in the sunny kitchen the next morning Delfina gave her a most disapproving look. In fact, two of them. One was because the hands of the clock indicated eleven. Delfina went to bed at eight and rose at five, she said, her strong face shining with the abominable virtue of the early and industrious riser.

The other was for her appearance. "The more you sleep, the worse you look, Miss Penny," she declared flatly.

As she went through the motions of eating the breakfast Delfina felt was good for her Penelope found it difficult to believe anything could have happened there. She tried to ask questions that would not break too incongruously into the scene. Had Delfina heard her come in last night? Had she heard her—and by that she meant anyone—fall on the veranda steps? Indeed Delfina had not. She went to bed to sleep. And did.

Was there really only one entrance to the Fabrica da Luz? Did the employees who lived in clusters of tiny houses she had noticed south of the property have to walk all the way round to the north gate?

Yes, they did, Delfina said shortly. That walk, morning and evening, was good for them—kept them from becoming fat and lazy.

"There is another gate, but it's private," she added.

Mr. Mart lived in the superintendent of ground's house, the last of a row of houses just outside the west wall. For his convenience a small iron gate had been cut through the Fabrica wall between his back garden and the factory grounds to give him immediate access if necessary. But he alone had the key to that little gate. And night and day three vicious dogs ranged between his locked front gate and that back one.

"But Mr. Mart is fiercer than one dog added to the other. No one would dare go in there, not even Mr. Paul, unless Mr. Mart went too." Delfina turned a startled eye on Penny. "Why?"

"Nothing," Penny assured her hastily. "Just listening to the rain last night, I wondered."

No, Delfina was not the one to confide in. Remained Wythe and Mart. Eleanor had recommended Wythe; Paul, Mart. But she did not feel up to facing Mart's derisive eyes and laughter. Wythe's quiet, understanding manner was infinitely preferable at a time like this.

"I've put the rug Dona Eleanor uses out by the Casa gates this morning," Delfina broke in. "But don't stay long, Miss Penny. It's almost noon and the sun's like fire."

Inwardly Penny groaned as she realized she must postpone her call on Dr. Sloane until after his luncheon hour. To fail to take a sun bath would merely set off more questions or protests from Delfina.

The rug was spread on the grass just off the driveway between the royal palms and the Casa. The Baroneza rushed wildly round it, then off to poke her nose into more hopeful spots in the hedge.

But Penny took no pleasure in the sunshine or in the lustrous crowns of palm fronds down which the sunlight slipped to sparkle like golden dew on each tip. All she could see were the Casa gates on one side, the veranda steps on the other. All she could think of were those gates and steps in darkness and rain.

She dropped down on the rug and slipped off her robe. The Baroneza, taking that as a signal she would be there some time, promptly curled up in the shade of a basket-sculptured shrub and went to sleep.

Penny could not relax with her. Wasn't it curious, she asked herself, that the Baroneza's busy nose had found no new scent as she romped about?

She sat up, then jumped up. A thought almost worse than the night's experience shot her through and through with apprehension. Could her wretched nerves have been playing tricks with her? Had she imagined that menacing rustle? That crumpled body? Those streaks of blood she had scouted from her hand?

The veranda steps were dry and spotless. The driveway from steps to gate had no answer. Through white gravel the red soil shone pink and clean except where shadows of mango trees spread changing patterns.

The Casa gates, swung back and fastened by their little wooden blocks, looked just as usual. The hedge, straight and smartly clipped, the firm path beneath damp leaves—to her inexperienced eyes, at least—gave no sign that any-one had stood there.

Seizing a short stick, she jumped down again and poked along the edge of the driveway between the Casa gates and veranda steps. She turned over leaves, thrust twigs and small pebbles out of the way. Nothing.

And then—just beside the steps—she saw in a dip in the earth where rain still stood a glint of metal, only a tiny glint, but something. With her stick she tipped it out of its pool to the drive and examined it. Picked it up and looked, again.

No such piece had ever come her way before. It had no practical purpose or value. It was not decorative enough to be worn as an ornament. But though she did not know what it might mean to anyone else, it was a heaven-sent sign to her.

On her hand lay a tiny metal cylinder of gold and silver. Not more than an inch long, it was carefully molded into a right arm and hand. The silver hand was doubled into a fist. The gold arm swelled out to just below the elbow, where it was cut off and sealed with gold.

A chain of four minute gold links clung to a loop set in the smooth top. The last of the four links that had been twisted or broken open.

With the little arm in her handkerchief Penelope arrived at the brown varnished doors of the laboratories shortly after two o'clock. At her knock a pleasant Brazilian girl opened them to her, and she stepped immediately into an office. Wythe Sloane, sitting at the desk there, quickly rose to greet her.

As she watched him approach, smiling, her heart sank. Perhaps she should have gone to Mart after all. This man looked so remote from contact with life beyond that quiet laboratory. How could he possibly understand what she had come to say?

She began clearly enough the story of her experience. But though his eyes retained their friendly interest, behind their surface, she could feel as she went on, he was analyzing her and her words. What was more, he was doubting them.

She hesitated, fumbled, repeated herself for emphasis, finally stopped when she saw one eyebrow lift as she told of the Casa gate closing of itself.

"You say this man was dead?" he asked after a moment. "How do you know? Perhaps, as you yourself thought at first, he had fallen and struck his head. Those tiles are hard as iron, you know. He may have recovered between the time you left him and returned to look out the window."

"He was dead. I know it. He couldn't have been alive. His head—the blood—" She could not describe what she had felt rather than seen.

"A little bit of blood can seem like an awful lot to a young woman on a dark and stormy night." When she remained silent he added, "Could you see what he looked like? How he was dressed? How large a man he was?"

Apparently these were serious questions, but she felt he was giving little attention to the answers. His attention was on her, not her words.

"It was dark—pouring rain—I couldn't really see. He wasn't a big man—at least he didn't seem big—"

"And the watchman didn't notice anything? Let's say you arrived back at the Casa about ten and were in the house when the watchman made his ten-o'clock round. That means he must have passed the Casa gates at least eight times before six o'clock this morning. He never stopped at all?"

"No."

Wythe picked up a chunk of rough glass from his desk and tumbled it back and forth in his hands, watching light from the high windows above him play over it. When he looked up his eyes were less skeptical, more concerned.

"Will you take some advice from me?"

He must have seen her strong inward reservation, for he did not begin with advice. "I know what you're going through," he said slowly. "I had a breakdown myself—several years ago. I know what nerves can do, what strange ideas they can put in your head. . . ."

"These aren't strange ideas," she interrupted. "I tell you I saw that man. I touched him. His—his blood was on my hand. Are you forgetting that someone else was there, too—waiting beside the hedge? I'm positive he frightened me so I wouldn't shut that gate."

She jumped up and turned for the doors. Words were futile before the skepticism in his face, his whole manner now.

He moved to the door with her and put out his hand. "Please don't go away feeling as you do. I do understand. And don't wander around the grounds after dark, though there is no danger, of course. It is impossible for anyone to enter. Wait a moment."

Picking up a desk phone, he dialed quickly. "Mart?" he asked after a moment. "Did the gate sheet record anyone entering the north gate last night? No? Were any accidents reported—a watchman or fireman injured?"

He replaced the receiver before he turned again to Penny. "No one entered the grounds last night after six o'clock. All the men who remained inside are intact. The gateman records the time each person arrives and leaves. You say you saw this man on the veranda steps about ten o'clock. If he came in before six the gateman would have notified the watchmen he had not been checked out. In four hours they could have found him a dozen times."

The telephone rang as he spoke. Before he lifted the receiver he stopped at Penny's chair to pick up something. She moved quickly and took the little gold-and-silver arm from his hand.

When he finished the call she held it out to him. "There. I found that beside the veranda steps."

Wythe turned it over in his hand, then smiled. "Don't you know what it is? It's a *figa*—a lucky charm—called the Protecting Arm or something like that. You'll see many of them when you begin to go about. Huge ones hanging in the doorways of small shops. Tiny ones like this about the necks and wrists of children. It protects Brazilians from the evil eye. Anyone might have lost this yesterday or a year ago. Though this is the first one I've seen in gold and silver. Usually they're made of *guiné* wood."

Not too politely Penny took it from him. "Then I'll keep it. I can use a little protection."

"Don't say that," he protested. "Perhaps you need amusement more than protection. Rio has beautiful scenic highways, and I have a car—"

"Thank you. I have the Olivers' car and José."

"What about movies? Rio has many of them, and good ones. And night clubs. Though you shouldn't go—"

"Yes, I should go," she interrupted, impatient to get away. "Good-by and thank you so much for listening."

"Let's say *até logo.*" He smiled at her through the closing door. "That means 'till soon.'"

"Self-centered idiot!" Penny hurried down the short path from his door to the pavement. "He didn't do a thing. Well, that's the last of him."

But he had done for her the one thing she needed most. His lack of belief had convinced her more than his credulity might have done of the reality of her experience. And he had made her so angry, she felt more energetic than she had for weeks. He would amuse her, would he? Tell her what she should and should not do!

She stopped to slip the little arm for safekeeping on the bar of her scarfpin and replace it securely. "Hereafter I'll depend on myself and amuse myself. And I'll start right now."

A few more determined steps and she stopped again. What could she do? Where could she go? The thought of returning to the Casa to be reminded on every hand of the night before was intolerable. She must get away from it, see other people, other scenes. But where? There was only Rio, and she couldn't go there.

Why not? She demanded obstinately of herself. She had traveled over India when five years younger than she was now. In some cities she had known no one, nor could she speak any of the various languages of the country.

Her hand closed about some coins in her pocket. She drew them out. Brazilian milreis she had received in change on the *Paraguay!* Surely they were a sign she should begin now, as she had said, to depend on herself and amuse herself.

Without pausing to return to the Casa to tell Delfina she was going, she hurried to the north gate.

9

Going to Rio—without a motorcar—was a simple but lengthy undertaking. Penny crossed the railway spur just beyond the factory wall, waved on by a fat signalman squeezed into a tiny shelter and urgent nods from an almost naked urchin who a moment later hurtled past her as if his scanty garment were on fire.

A right turn onto the gravel road, a five minutes' walk under the bright scrutiny of women and children in the boxlike houses brought her to the tracks of the main line. The crossing gates were closed. Above, in a tower, a signalman jumped from lever to lever like a caged canary among its perches.

Minutes passed. Two or three soldiers went round the gates and on. Penelope waited with the gathering cars, trucks, and oxcarts.

Free at last to cross, she made her way through small boys flying kites, groups of soldiers off duty, and gnarled cluster of dogs to the junction with the main highway.

Two methods of transportation offered—an open streetcar and an airtight bus. She chose the streetcar.

Her enthusiasm and energy for the venture were beginning to wane. Though only a handful of passengers were scattered among the seats that ran from side to side of the car, those few took a detailed interest in everything about her.

One young man in a crumpled linen suit and heavy black fedora had rushed up, pulling on a jacket as he ran. Seating himself in front of her on the other side of the car, he eyed her with the shiny glance of the professional lady's man.

Absorbed shortly in the changing sights of the narrow, cobbled streets, she did not notice that the young man in the fedora had slid nearer. Only when she tired of a street of shops whose doorways were almost impassable with shoes or garlic suspended on cords did she become conscious of his eyes. They were fastened on her scarfpin. She smiled to herself. The pin was large and impressive but of no value really.

The car stopped. The motorman descended to release the trolley. As other passengers scrambled off the conductor's hands invited her to do the same or return with the car. Rested now, she descended and, following the majority of passengers, found herself shortly on Rio's most famous street, the Avenida Rio Branco.

A hundred feet wide, its broad sidewalks laid in black-and-white mosaics, it was faced on both sides by stone buildings. Wide lanes, separated by aisles of banyan trees, roared with traffic.

Far ahead against the familiar outline of Sugar Loaf Mountain an obelisk, marking the end of the avenue, challenged her. But she never reached it. Interesting as the mosaic sidewalks were to the eyes, they were something else to the feet.

The appearance of sidewalk cafés was a welcome sight. Selecting an advantageous table in the inside corner of one of them, she dropped into a prickly wicker chair. "Lemonade," she said to a waiter. *"Limonada,"* he corrected with great expertness and disappeared into the café behind her.

Sipping her chaste drink, she lingered while the daily promenade of smart and not so smart men and women passed and repassed. The personnel at the small tables changed, but the glint of diamonds on hands and wrists, ears, frocks, hats, and shirt fronts remained constant. Dr. Attilio was right, she agreed. Diamonds in Brazil were almost as numerous as coffee beans.

Her spirits rose as she found interest and amusement in everything. But fell with a crash when she looked up to find a dapper young man approaching her table. Senhor Rodrigo!

Before she could rise he had swung an empty chair round from a neighboring table and seated himself in it. As he fixed his black eyes on her, her fingers sought the Brazilian coins in her pocket and her eyes a waiter, any waiter.

"Do not be disturbed, Miss Paget," he said in very good English. "I only wish to speak with the senhorita for one minute."

"Certainly not." She tried to rise.

"See, you cannot leave until I leave also, Miss Paget. And that will be when you consent to talk with me here— or elsewhere."

Penelope looked around. Across the high railing on her left, separating her from the next café, no one was even looking in her direction. On the sidewalk the promenaders appeared completely immersed in their own affairs. Besides, they were all Brazilians—might not speak English. If only someone with an English or American face would come along!

She saw with dismay that the street lamps were flashing on, that her corner was now dim and secluded. Even if someone did come could she be seen?

Senhor Rodrigo, watching, smiled. "It is difficult, is it not? But I merely wish to ask two little questions."

Penny, gazing over his head, smiled too. Mart's unmistakable red head—hatless and rumpled—had appeared for

a moment above the strollers approaching. She sat forward, waiting.

But as he came opposite his name died on her lips. His
eyes met hers directly, passed over her, without a sign of
recognition. The next moment he was gone.

Really alarmed now, she sat quiet. On Rio's main avenue, crowded with people, surely it was impossible for
Senhor Rodrigo to isolate and detain her. With relief she
remembered Delfina. If she didn't return soon Delfina
might send José to look for her!

Paper rustled on the table before her. She looked down
to see the flimsy of a wireless in Senhor Rodrigo's outstretched hand.

"Read it, please," he was saying. "You cannot, perhaps?
Then I will read it for you. It was sent by Dr. Rosario to a
kinsman in Rio the afternoon our ship reached Barbados."

Kinsman! Barbados! The two words clicked together in
Penelope's mind. Dr. Rosario had left the SS *Paraguay* at
Barbados and never returned. Dr. Attilio had said a kins-
man of his had been found mysteriously dead in Barbados.
Could Dr. Rosario be the kinsman?

"Miss Paget, you will listen, please? The wireless reads:
'In case my arrival delayed see passenger Penelope Paget
destination Rio concerning Fouché.'"

Penelope scarcely heard the words. She was seeing again
the gentle Dr. Rosario escaping hurriedly from her cabin.
Could it have been the diamond he was seeking? Could
Fouché be his code word for it? Could it have been the
diamond—the Fouché—that others, Senhor Rodrigo and
the false Dr. Rosario, had been seeking those days when she
found her cabin disturbed? Had they killed that kind old
man when he failed and undertaken the search themselves?

She looked back at Senhor Rodrigo as coldly as he had
ever looked at her. And now he dared to come to her openly to ask about that diamond!

"You will tell me what you know about Fouché?" His voice was low but insistent. "It is necessary, Miss Paget. A man's life depends on my knowing. It is already late—"

"Too late!"

The words burst from Penny's lips against her will. She shrank back in her chair, aghast at her foolhardiness. Aghast, too, at the certainty in her mind that Dr. Rosario—the real Dr. Rosario—was dead. She had only suspected until she met Senhor Rodrigo's eyes just now. Now she knew!

And he knew that she knew. He had leaned forward, his black eyes narrowed and icy on hers. "Too late?" he was repeating softly. "What are you saying, Miss Paget?"

Penelope bent her head and twisted the broken straws about her glass with shaking fingers. Her mind was frozen before the arctic menace she felt in his.

"Miss Paget!"

Another voice—a brisk, authoritative voice—was speaking her name. She looked up to see another slender, dark man, hat in hand, smiling at her over Senhor Rodrigo's head. As she gazed at him with mingled misgiving and hope he turned to speak rapidly yet courteously to Senhor Rodrigo, then look about for an empty chair.

Senhor Rodrigo rose slowly, gesturing to his own as he replied in Portuguese. He turned then to smile with his lips at Penelope. *Até logo,* Miss Paget, I look forward to seeing you again."

"How delightful to find you here," the newcomer was saying. "I have only now learned you are in Rio." As Senhor Rodrigo still lingered in the entrance to the café he dropped into the vacated chair to ask, "What are you drinking? *Limonada?* You will have one with me?"

Penny shook her head, her eyes wary. When Senhor Rodrigo had gone she asked, "Who—who are you?"

Her new companion smiled. "In your country you have a flattering word for men like me. Intelligence! And am I not of the intelligence? I pass this café, observe your predicament, and arrive to do the necessary."

"You are a detective?"

"If you like. But your friend has gone. Come, my car is just at the corner. I must take you home."

"No, no," she protested, alarmed again. "If you really want to help me, please telephone my house. The chauffeur will come in for me."

"That would be delightful if hours were days. But I can have you at the Fabrica gates before he could possibly arrive here. Come, Miss Paget."

He stood up, and she had to rise too. There was no mistaking the authority in his voice and manner. He paid her check and led her silently to his car. As silently they sped down the Avenida. Stiff with uneasiness, she sat upright until familiar landmarks convinced her he was really taking her home.

"Ah, that is better." He gave her an amused smile. "A few minutes more and you will see the Fabrica wall. Let me advise you a little before I leave you. Quite innocently, I am sure, you have walked into a very complicated situation in Rio. Even dangerous for a young woman here alone. It is most unfortunate that the Olivers—had to leave unexpectedly."

"What situation, Senhor—? I'm sorry, I do not know your name."

"Let us hope you never know it. If you will do as I suggest and remain within the Fabrica walls for a few days you may not need to. Or to know about—the situation, either. We hope to end it shortly. Then you will be quite free to go where you will."

He swung off the main highway onto the gravel road before he spoke again. "See? You are almost on your own doorstep. Can you trust me now to tell me what you know about Fouché?"

Startled, she shook her head. He smiled. "So that was what your friend on the Avenida wished to know also? Perhaps for the same reason."

"But I know no one named Fouché—"

"Naturally. I believe the gentleman referred to lived in the days of the French Revolution. Does that mean anything to you?"

She flushed a little. "Only that he was the sort of man to sit on both sides of the fence and in the middle—"

"A little knowledge is not enough, is it? A pity. But no matter. At the moment." He swung left and stopped the car before the north gate. "Here you are."

Penelope's eyes darkened with anger instead of gratitude. For the light above the gatehouse revealed Mart just inside the gates. He was talking to the little old Negro gateman.

Now he hurried forward as the gateman unlocked the gates, thrust them back. "Miss Paget! Fancy meeting you here! I thought you were sleeping the clock round in the Casa."

His glance went on to the detective, and they talked briefly in Portuguese. "Your friend has already devoted more time than he had to spare to bring you here," he told Penny then. "So I have consented to see you safely home from this point."

Penny sprang to the ground, close to tears, as she felt rather than saw the amusement they were both enjoying at her expense. "Thank you," she tried to say with dignity. "It isn't necessary for either of you—"

Mart drew her aside as the detective's car backed and shot away. And he continued to stand, a restraining hand on her arm, as he looked after it, whistling under his breath. "Do you see what I see?"

Penny tried to draw away. "I don't believe I'm interested. Good night."

"Listen, my peppery little *Americana!*" Mart's long strides kept pace with her hurried steps. "You're in Brazil now, where men have a word or two to say. I'm taking you to your own door—not a step farther. And heaven help you if you don't stay there. While I'm at it, another word of courteous counsel. Keep away from that American smoothie, Wythe Sloane. If you must weep on someone's shoulder come to mine."

Penny jerked herself free. "What do you mean?"

"Oh, I saw you when you left his office. An amateur April, that's what you were. Splashing all over the place!"

"That's not true. I mean, you couldn't have seen me. You were in your office. Wythe telephoned you there."

"You think I'm paralyzed? I galloped over pronto to see what roused that fellow's interest in the welfare of my employees. And what did I see? You!"

"Odd your eyes were so good then but couldn't see me on the avenue this afternoon!"

"This afternoon? On the Avenida? My little tiger lily. I'm a workingman."

Seizing her arm, he rushed her up some rough earthen steps cut into the hill to a more or less flat plateau. Through the high dry grass that covered it various paths converged on the steps.

"I'll go ahead. Follow me."

Eager to reach the Casa, Penny did follow, running in her effort to keep up with him. Mart led her round by the watchman's path to the Casa gates and in to the veranda.

"Boa noite," he said politely. "And don't thank me. I'd do anything for Paul."

"Paul?"

"Paul. He gave me this job when Mario Soares left it between night and day some months ago, and I'm going to keep it. One way is to keep you out of trouble."

"Oh, stop talking nonsense," Penny cried, exasperated. "Did you know that man who brought me home?"

"Who? Me? Duchess, I have no social life whatever."

"Then why did you say, 'Do you see what I see?' when he backed his car out of the north gate?"

For once Mart appeared at a loss. Then he looked at her squarely. "I was just wondering who else was taking an interest in your reaching the Fabrica."

"Who else? You mean you were?"

He shouted with laughter. "What big ideas you have, grandma. No, what I saw was the glow of a cigarette in the darkness beside that railway-crossing shelter. It just occurred to me someone was interested Maybe not—"

Abruptly he was serious. "Penny, Paul's in a tight spot. And through no fault of his own. You've caused enough trouble, sending him off like that to New York. The least you can do is to keep out of Rio."

"Keep out of Rio?"

"Why not? All of us—Cock, Dr. Attilio, even your little Wythe—have all covered up for him. So you go to Rio alone. Mightn't that suggest to anyone interested that Paul and Eleanor are not here?"

"Don't be ridiculous! No one in Rio knows I exist."

"No? What made this Brazilian Galahad tote you home? Now I'm going to tell you something and I mean it. Stay inside the Fabrica walls. Have anyone you like—or don't like, for that matter, meaning me—at the Casa. But don't go outside. *Claro?*"

"I assume you mean clear. Perfectly. Now what do I do? Send out balloons to drop messages asking someone to come in? If I stay here alone day and night I'll begin muttering to myself."

"Oh, good night!" Mart strode away.

For a moment Penny listened to his irritated footsteps on the graveled path round the house. Then reluctantly, dreading the long evening and night ahead, she opened the doors and entered the living room.

10

While she bathed and changed for dinner Delfina hovered close, concealing relief under irritation. "Where have you been, Miss Penny?" she demanded over and over. "I looked everywhere for you, and Dr. Wythe scolded me for letting you go out alone. He has telephoned many times since five o'clock."

"I've been to London to see the King." Penelope concealed her own irritation under flippancy. With Wythe, Mart, even this detective telling her what to do, she might as well be in New York with Andrea and Pepperpot.

"Brazil has a president," Delfina corrected her. "And you can't speak Portuguese. Why didn't you take José and the car? Dr. Wythe thought something had happened to you."

Penny was alarmed at the violence of her own reaction. It was a danger signal, she knew, warning her of nerves stretched to the breaking point. "Serve dinner," she said shortly. "I'll be there in a moment."

The food or wine or misgivings at the thought of facing the evening alone excited her still further. She kept Delfina beside her in the dining room, chattering to her feverishly. When the maid left the room without explanation Penny looked penitently at the Baroneza stretched out in the archway, even her bright eyes anxious.

"Don't mind me, Baroness. I guess I'm just tired or lonely or something. I never thought to hear myself saying this, but I'd give Satan's Sixth Finger if you could turn into Pepperpot for just an hour."

Delfina came in with a note the gateman had sent up. "For you, Miss Penny," she said, turning it over uneasily. "But you don't know anyone in Rio."

"That's what you think!" Penelope muttered to herself as she took the cheap white envelope.

On the outside was written "Miss Pagee" and on equally cheap paper inside but in more literate handwriting:

> *By this you can see I KNow English but not good so it is a big pleasure to know you are come and perhaps to help me speak better. I could like to learn as I am Hindu and so enthuse I could come tonite. If you are so kind telephon 29-0009 and so I come there.*
> *Your firend,*
> *Mr. Mukerji*

Delfina's reaction was both definite and amusing. "Tear it up," she urged, her chin thrust out. "Tear it up, Miss Penny. Why does he want you to teach him? He can get many teachers in Rio."

"It might be interesting," Penelope teased. "I lived for a year in India, you know. Certainly it wouldn't be difficult."

"No, Miss Penny. If he comes he must come in the day. It is not right to see him at night. If he knows you are here he knows you are alone."

"Nonsense. He doesn't want to come to call. This is business in a way. And I know many people in India. He may be a friend of one of them."

"Mr. Paul and the senhora lived many years in India. He does not try to see them. Besides"—Delfina paused to marshal her big guns into action—"Dr. Wythe and Mr. Mart would not like it."

That changed the picture. Penny regarded the maid with serious eyes.

"Do you know what an issue is, Delfina? This is one. All day long people—Dr. Wythe, Mr. Mart, and—and others—have been telling me what not to do. Perhaps I'm set in my ways. Perhaps I'm too accustomed to making decisions for myself and other people. And now here I am— in a strange country, among strangers—and with so many things happening. I mean everything is so different here," she corrected hastily.

"I'm growing confused, Delfina, and uncertain of myself. Yet with Mr. Paul and the senhora away, I must rely on myself. Don't you see? If I don't decide things for myself, even if I make mistakes, I'll just become more confused or uncertain—and I won't get better. I'll get worse."

"No, I don't see, Miss Penny," Delfina told her stoutly. "You can't make a mistake if you don't do anything. About that letter, I mean. You just don't like to have people tell you what to do. Nobody does. I do not like you to say, 'Delfina, serve dinner.'"

Penelope startled them both by laughing with pure pleasure.

Delfina's smile grew into a laugh, too. Baroneza bounced up, plume waving, to rise on her hind legs and applaud with her front paws.

Delfina laughed again. "Now you must give her something to eat. She always does that when people laugh. Mr. Paul says she thinks they are admiring her."

When the Baroneza was rewarded tension was gone from the air and from Penny. The letter, forgotten for the moment, had lost its importance when she picked it up again.

"Do you know what I think, Delfina? I believe this 'Mr. Mukerji' is just a young boy. Probably feeling as strange and lonely here as I do. A man never would have signed a letter like that. He would have written out his full name. I've known a lot of Hindu boys—so simple and friendly and eager to learn. Why, it might be fun to have him here. Imagine teaching a young Hindu English in a South American country that speaks Portuguese."

You fraud, she scolded herself, you know you're afraid of being alone all evening. You're worse than a fraud. You're a fool. And a bully. But she could not control the perverse excitement that gripped her.

"I'll make a bargain with you, Delfina," she said finally. "We'll have him here and you can sit in the living room with us and hear all and see all. If he is not what I think he is I'll give you—what would you like of mine?"

The dark face became a battleground between disapproval and desire. Then a spark kindled in the large eyes. "Your black coat, Miss Penny."

"Done. Will you please call that number, Delfina? Tell Mr. Mukerji he can come from half-past eight to nine."

At half-past eight exactly Mr. Mukerji arrived. A self-important little man whose strong black hair stood up in arches from its middle part, he was anything but the simple boy Penelope had visualized.

Behind large steel-rimmed glasses his eyes roamed constantly, and at times the narrow lobes of his ears twitched. Penny never did learn whether the sleeves of his sleazy, too-bright blue suit were too long or too short. His small, apparently boneless hands kept shooting in and out of his cuffs as he talked.

"Good night," he greeted Penelope, crossing the room to her and holding out his hand in a combination of cordiality and obsequiousness that cramped her anticipation then and there. "You are so kind to teach me. I am truly one good pupil. I know many English words to see in a book. I only don't talk them correct."

His accent was strange, unlike any Penny had heard in India. And he spoke very rapidly, his eyes searching her and the room and Delfina indiscriminately. He sat down in one of the big overstuffed chairs under a lamp but, when it almost swallowed him, moved forward hastily to perch on the edge.

"First we must talk the cost."

Conscious of Delfina sitting upright on a straight chair across the room in an attitude that at the same time achieved triumph and grim watchfulness, Penny's reply was prompt. "Oh, I don't know that I can teach you, Mr. Mukerji. I let you come tonight to find out."

"You think I am poor?" The small hands dug out a bill-fold. "See? I pay any cost."

"Suppose we try reading first," Penny suggested, determined that this was his first and last lesson. "That will give me an idea of your pronunciation and vocabulary."

A rack of Eleanor's household magazines stood beside her chair. She drew one out and offered it to him. He looked at the tanned body of a girl in a bathing suit extended in a dive through sky and sea across its cover.

"Excuse, but I am a man," he said finally, putting it on the floor. "I must read books—serious words. Poli*tics*, *eco*nomics, his*to*ry. You have?"

"How would this do?" Penny picked up the only one of her own books she had carried in her bags, *The All-American Front.*

"Ah," he murmured, rising to take it. "Good. You like such books? You have more?"

"Those I brought with me include a little of everything."

"How inter*est!* I could see?" Again he was up, looking about.

"Not tonight. I haven't opened them—"

"You must!" he cried. Then at her surprise lowered his voice. "We starve in Rio for books from your country. They are most difficult to have."

"We cannot get them," Delfina's flat voice declared with finality. "They are on a high shelf."

"But I am a man," he reminded them again. "I can—"

This was too much. "Not tonight." Penny's voice was crisp. "Will you begin to read?"

"Yes, yes." He subsided on his chair edge, opened the book.

He read well because he read slowly. Except for mistakes right and left with accents, he seemed to know, as he had said, many English words.

Penny relaxed little by little. While one part of her mind roused occasionally to correct Mukerji's pronunciation, another drifted away to thoughts of its own.

Why had Wythe Sloane called her several times? Been so concerned about her absence? Was it Wythe who had sent Mart to watch for her at the north gate? Or Delfina?

She smiled to herself at Mart's description of the chemist. In every way the two were antagonistic types. Remembering her own exasperation with Wythe that afternoon, she could appreciate his effect on the active, aggressive Mart. One thing she would not think about. Senhor Rodrigo and his low, chilled voice repeating, "Too late?"

Her ear suddenly called her back to focus on Mukerji's reading. "Please read that paragraph again," she suggested and, when his glance questioned her, added lamely, "You read very well. I'm afraid I was thinking of the context, not your pronunciation."

He read the paragraph again. Listening, Penelope forced herself to remain relaxed in her chair. This man was not in need of English instruction from her or anyone. He knew the meaning and pronunciation of every word he read. In the quiet he, too, had relaxed, mispronouncing a word one way one time, a different way when he met it again. Her ear had caught what her mind had missed.

Mukerji, also, she could see, was forcing himself to concentrate. Was he trying to remember how he had mispronounced these words originally? Was his spoken and written English all just one big pretense, too? Why had he really come?

She caught her breath. Could he have some association with Rodrigo? What a fool she had been to allow pique against Wythe and Mart to override her judgment!

Five minutes to nine, said the clock above the fireplace. She listened a little longer, made careful corrections, then rose. Mukerji closed the book and lifted himself from his cramped position. Behind his glasses his eyes were winking rapidly.

"I am so thankful," he began. "I have learn—"

"You don't need to be," Penny assured him. "You do very well and should find a professional teacher to give you English grammar. I wouldn't know a participle if I saw one."

"But you are most good," he insisted, taking a few short steps across the floor. "I come tomorrow."

Delfina had risen too. Mukerji made no further move toward the door. Penelope's disturbed impression that he wasn't the fool he looked became definite. He expected to see someone or something here!

"We'll call this lesson a sample," she said, going to the doors and opening them wide, pointedly. "If I decide to continue I'll let you know. Good night."

He moved toward her slowly, Delfina now close on his heels, her mouth grim. At the doors he paused again, measuring them and the room.

Then unaccountably, at a sound on the veranda, he stepped outside and hurried away. Both Penny and Delfina peered out to see what had moved him when they could not.

Stretched out in a lounge chair, tapping his pipe on the metal rim of the ash tray, was Wythe Sloane.

He greeted them, getting up. Delfina sniffed. "I was afraid to take my eyes off that fellow. He was scared of something too."

"Nonsense, Delfina," Penny protested. "Though he did come under false pretenses. What do you suppose he really wanted?"

"He wanted to go all round this house. Dr. Wythe, he tried to go into Miss Penny's room and get her books."

"He did spoil a good evening, didn't he?"

"Good night!" Delfina marched into the house.

Penny moved across the veranda to look out over the valley to the mountains, silent and dark except where fires burned like angry eyes high on their slopes. Wythe followed to stand beside her.

"What are you looking at so intently?"

"The fires. See? Four, five—at least six of them. Don't the Brazilians like their country?"

"Oh, they're just burning over dead grass and underbrush. One way to keep down mosquitoes and snakes. Thanks for reminding me. I must ask Mart to have the grass above the laboratories burned off Saturday. The mosquito men were fussing about it last week."

"Mosquito men!"

"Haven't you seen them? You will. They come round every week, looking for standing water and other mosquito breeding spots. To prevent malaria, yellow fever, and what not. Doing a good job too."

His casual tone changed. "I came up tonight for several reasons. We got off to a bad start this afternoon, didn't we?"

"It doesn't matter," Penny tried to say lightly. "Naturally you didn't believe me."

"I didn't believe you, I admit—then." Wythe stressed the word and paused. "But I'm beginning to change my mind."

Penny turned to look at him. His face in the dim light was tired and worried. "Why?" she asked quickly.

"I'd rather not say yet. But I'd like to hear that story again with every detail you can think of. Do you mind? And let's talk in the Casa."

This time he listened to every word, stopping her again and again for additional details of time and place and sounds. When she finished he asked, "Do you still have that little gold arm with the silver hand?"

"Of course I have. I'm going to keep it as long as I can."

"Would five minutes be long enough? I've brought you a real one—of *guiné* wood—instead." He fished a tiny packet out of his pocket.

Penny looked curiously at the little wooden model, then gave it back. "Thanks, no. This isn't the same as mine."

He laughed and refused to take it. "Certainly it is. They're all alike."

"Wait a minute."

She brought out her scarfpin, slipped the little gold arm from its bar, and placed it on his hand beside the *guiné* arm. At first glance most people would have said they were the same. Side by side under the reading lamp, however, they revealed several differences.

Hers was the mold of a right arm and hand. His, of the left. Hers had the hand doubled threateningly into a fist, the thumb pressing against the forefinger and projecting a little above it. The fingers of the *guiné* hand were smoothly folded; the thumb, inserted between the first and second fingers, projected a little above. Then, of course, hers was of gold and silver; his, of this feather-weight wood generally used, as he had said.

Wythe Sloane whistled. "The plot thickens, as someone has said so well."

"Tell me what you know," Penny suggested. "Something must be done about this. People can't go around murdering other—"

"Don't be so American," he advised. "And don't jump to conclusions."

"I've told you twice what I know."

"And I'll tell you what I know—when I know it, or in politer words to that effect. If you'll let me take your Protecting Arm—your Unprotecting Arm, I should say— perhaps I can tell you tomorrow."

"What are you going to do with it? Use it in some sort of test?" At his nod she protested, "But you can't do that. You might destroy it. It's evidence. And, besides, I want it. It is a Protecting Arm. It protected me today."

He looked up sharply. "What happened today?"

She regretted her impulsive words. "Oh, nothing, really. I was jumping to conclusions, as you say."

"That doesn't make sense. Suppose you begin with the moment you left my office and tell me exactly what you saw, heard, and did until I arrived here tonight. I mean it," he declared when she looked dismayed. "For a young woman in Rio to rest, you have had a strenuous forty-eight hours. What has happened to both of us may hang together or may not. At any rate, tell me."

It was late and she was tired. With a start she saw that the clock marked almost exactly twenty-four hours since she had climbed the hill to find that body on the veranda steps. She tried to protest again, could not utter a word.

"I know what time it is and what's on your mind," Wythe assured her. "I'm not going home and leave you here to have the jitters by yourself. And I want to know what happened this afternoon. Let's get through the next hour or two by talking it over quietly."

Penny went into minute detail. But he asked for more.

"This youngster beside the railway shelter outside the north gate—you say he passed you, running. Did he stop to play in the street anywhere or go into a house or shop? Where did the young man in the fedora come from? You say he came running up. Do you think there is any connection between the running boy and running man?"

And later: "You say this young man—let's call him Fedora, for short—stared at your scarfpin. Are you sure it was the pin? Perhaps the Unprotecting Arm wasn't as well hidden as you thought. And you have no idea who your Brazilian was?"

Penny shook her head. She didn't feel up to telling Wythe about Rodrigo and all that had happened aboard the *Paraguay,* for one thing. For another, she felt that Dr. Attilio, if anyone, should be the first to hear her suspicions and certainties concerning that voyage. And finally something about Wythe's persistence disturbed her. Especially when he would tell her nothing of what he knew or thought himself.

"Fedora could have followed me up the Avenida to that café, then told the Brazilian where I was," she admitted wearily. "But I didn't see him. I wasn't thinking about him."

But his questions gave her no rest. "Perhaps Fedora was the man Mart saw beside the shelter when you returned. Perhaps there is a connection between Fedora and this man who was here tonight."

"Mukerji!" She opened her eyes, startled. "Could there be? Fedora was a Brazilian as far as I could see. Mukerji said he was Hindu."

"He might be anything. Something like forty or more nationalities are married and intermarried in Brazil. You must have noticed the endless mixtures on the Avenida."

Wythe sat forward again. "Delfina says Mukerji was afraid of something. You say you think he was here to see someone or something. Perhaps you're both right. Delfina usually knows what she is talking about, and your reasoning about his inconsistent pronunciations and roving eyes sounds logical. Let's begin with the tangible thing or what seems tangible. What could he have wanted?"

With an effort Penny kept her face a blank. What could he have wanted but that little clay elephant! Yet no one could expect to find it here now. If he knew she had had it he must know for whom it was intended. Must know it had reached its destination.

She thought of that dinner party—the eyes recording Dr. Attilio's ill-concealed satisfaction. Wythe and the Cochranes had been in this living room when Dr. Attilio and his wife arrived. Wythe and Mart and his mother had outstayed the others. Wythe! Could he have watched, reported? Could it be Wythe?

She sat up uneasily, expecting to find him watching her. But he was not in his chair or in the room. To her surprise she heard him in the kitchen, heard the refrigerator door click and the motor whir on. Doors of cupboards opening and shutting. Then he was in the dining room, coming toward her with a tray in his hands.

"You looked and I felt as if food were indicated." Placing the tray on the low table before her couch, he opened and poured cold beer, turned back a napkin to reveal sandwiches. "Delfina left them ready."

Seating himself, he lifted his glass. "Cheer up, thoughtful lady. Shall I tell you a story while we eat—though not as fascinating as Dr. Attilio's? It might light a gleam in your mental darkness."

"It's your turn. My tongue is fringed from talking."

"Well, about a year ago," he began, "Dr. Attilio told Paul and Eleanor part of that story about Satan's Sixth Finger. He understood the difficulties and dangers involved if he were to try to go to London himself to get it.

"So he invited Paul to have a part in it. Paul was to get the diamond and handle the financial end of it. You know Paul. He wouldn't cross the street to pick up a million if it took him away from his precious glassmaking for forty seconds.

"He refused—politely—and advised Dr. Attilio to leave the stone where it was until this war is over."

Wythe paused to munch a sandwich and study Penny appraisingly before he continued. "You probably know Eleanor better than I do. Know how completely wrapped up she is in Jay and sympathizes with his passion to live in the States, to have a permanent home, friends, roots."

"Help! You've lost Dr. Attilio somewhere."

"I'm coming to him. But Jay first. Just think of the poor kid. Born in Japan, educated in India and England, now living here. But he knows more about his own country, I'll bet, than thousands of fellows his age who live there. He's a fine chap and an excellent glassman, but his mind isn't on anything really but living in his own country.

"You don't need to convince me. He used to take me apart in India on everything from Coney Island to presidential elections."

"Well, though Paul refused to take up Dr. Attilio's offer, Eleanor didn't. If this stone is half as good as Dr. Attilio thinks it is, it must be worth in the rough between a half and three quarters of a million dollars. That ain't hay, as the American half of your friend Mart would say."

Penny put up an unsteady hand and touched the soft bob that had hidden a fortune for almost three weeks.

Wythe noticed the gesture. "To make it short, Eleanor and Dr. Attilio got together. Jay was to go to London with the proper credentials. Eleanor and Jay would receive a percentage of its sale price. Just how much I don't know, but to Eleanor it represented a permanent home in the States. I think she even hoped to persuade Paul to retire! That all clear?"

Penny nodded.

"Well, the diamond is here," Wythe declared. "And Jay isn't. By a curious coincidence it seems to have arrived on the very day you did."

Penny bent forward to set her glass down carefully. "How wonderful!" were the only words that came to her.

"For Dr. Attilio, yes. What about Jay?"

"What about Jay?"

"I'm asking you."

"I don't know. I don't know where Jay is."

"No? Well, I do. He must be in New York. The diamond came in on the New York boat."

"How do you know all this?" she demanded suddenly. "And why are you telling me? I—I think this is something Paul or Eleanor should have told me—if they had wanted me to know."

"I know most of it from Eleanor," Wythe said quietly. "Paul knew nothing of Jay's going until he was gone. Then he was sunk—as you can imagine. So was Eleanor, when she realized, too late, what might happen to him. For hours I've figuratively held her hand while she waited and worried to hear from him."

Wythe rose to light the cigarette Penny had picked up and to light his own.

"Much of the rest I've figured out from a word dropped here and there. Anyone knowing what I know could have deduced from Dr. Attilio's manner that something very pleasing had happened.

"Now planes arrive in the morning. And Tuesday noon he looked like something on a hot griddle. The *Paraguay*

docked in the afternoon—with the diamond, obviously—
and you."

When she gave no sign of understanding the implication in his words he went on, "I'm telling you all this because I think you should realize you are in this up to the ears. I'm not the only one who believes you brought the diamond down. And not the only one who believes you must have brought something else—information, possibly; I don't know. Anyway, something that has a vital bearing on this stone."

Penny remained silent, stroking the sleeping Baroneza beside her.

"Use your head," he said sharply. "Do you imagine every young woman who arrives in Brazil has experiences like yours? Why not admit you brought Satan's Sixth Finger and information or a message? We've got to find it before someone else is—"

"Murdered?" Penny looked up quickly. "You do believe me now?"

11

Wythe rose to draw his chair directly in front of her. "Let's not use that word—yet. But this is the way it looks to me.

"You arrived Tuesday afternoon. The Olivers left at dawn Wednesday morning. Wednesday evening someone tried to reach this house. Someone else tried to stop him. Does that suggest anything to you? Remember, several people suspected by that time that Dr. Attilio had the diamond."

"You mean you think it's this information—message—they believe to be here?"

"Just that. It took about twenty-four hours either to discover where you were or that you have whatever it is they want."

"But that's ridiculous. I haven't even got what I want myself. Just my own personal things, that's all."

"Money, jewelry, secret papers?"

"My money is in a letter of credit on a Rio bank. I've not even drawn on it yet. I don't care for jewelry and haven't any anyway. Papers? Some stationery and cleansing tissues—"

"What about clothes? Did you buy anything new before you left New York? send anything to tailors or cleaners? Could anyone who handled any of your things have slipped something into linings or hems without your knowing it?"

Penny heard him speaking, but her attention was far away—in the little passage that led to her cabin on the *Paraguay*. Seeing her door open inch by inch, then Dr. Rosario stepping out, to hurry away—book in hand.

"Penny!" Wythe was shaking her arm. "Are you asleep or ill?"

"Neither. I was just remembering something."

Penny's thoughts raced. She must be careful to avoid mention of Dr. Rosario, and Barbados.

"I forgot—about my books," she explained. "I brought in a package of books—"

"Books!" Wythe jumped up. "Who gave them to you? Where are they? You said Mukerji wanted to see them. Of course. Come on, let's get them."

But they didn't get them. The Baroneza, stiff-legged on the couch, was barking her small head off.

"What next?" Wythe hurried to the door. There a hesitant hand clapping, the Brazilian equivalent for a doorbell, was growing louder and more insistent.

Penny followed him to see the old Negro gateman shuffling his feet on the veranda and bowing apologetically.

At sight of Wythe he was clearly relieved and burst into a jumble of Portuguese.

From his repetitions of senhorita Americana and oblique glances in her direction Penny knew his coming concerned her. At last with more bows the old man shuffled away.

"It's about Mukerji, isn't it?" she prompted when they turned back to the living room. "But they can't have been holding that poor idiot at the north gate for three hours!"

"They haven't been holding Mukerji at the gate for three hours. They've been expecting him for three hours. He hasn't appeared."

"That's impossible!" Penny cried. "That old Haile must have been sleeping and a watchman let Mukerji out. No, that's impossible, too, I suppose. But why did they wait three hours to investigate?"

"At first thought Mukerji had stayed longer than expected, you being young and, shall we say, charming? And the watchman after his ten- and eleven-o'clock rounds told him you were still up and someone here. Then Haile became concerned—thought perhaps you needed someone. He had to wait, however, for a watchman to return to relieve him at the gate. He was darned glad to find it was I who was keeping you up."

"What did you tell him to do?"

"To do nothing. If anything out of the ordinary seems to be happening on the grounds the watchman will call Mart. Lord! I hope nothing gets that human ferret out of bed. If the watchmen report nothing I told Haile to come back here when he goes off duty."

Wythe moved restlessly round the room, crushing out one cigarette, lighting another.

"Look here," he said finally. "Something's up and I'm worried. About your being here alone. About Paul being away—"

"You're not telling me everything."

"He said and he didn't mean to; it slipped out because the poor devil's in a panic about losing his job—that this was the second time a man had come in the north gate and had not been checked out. When I asked him about the first time he crawfished, said it was weeks ago. I think he lied. I think it was last night. I think it was the man you saw lying on the Casa steps." He stopped short. "Or the man responsible for his being there."

Penny took a deep breath but felt relieved too. There was no doubt that Wythe believed her story now.

"What do we do about it?"

"That's what I'm trying to decide. Perhaps I should take you in to stay with the Cochranes. Perhaps I should tell Cock—"

"He mightn't believe you any more than you believed me this afternoon," Penny interposed hastily. "We still have nothing but that Unprotecting Arm. And you laughed that off."

"That's what stops me, for one thing. Another is that Cock might turn everything over to the police. That wouldn't be pleasant for you or me personally, and it might bring the New York office down on our heads—and Paul's—"

"Paul's! That simply can't happen."

"Take it easy," he advised. "All this could have happened, I suppose, even if he had been here. It begins to look as if something were happening—or had been for some time."

"Nothing happened until I came. You said that yourself."

"That's true. But you may be just a—a lighted match tossed into dry grass."

He was talking to himself more than to Penny, thinking out loud. She remained quiet and waited. She had plenty to think about herself.

Wythe might be right about something going on under the surface. At least if what he had said about the existence of the diamond was true, wasn't it curious that Dr. Attilio should have denied so elaborately that it existed at all? And if it was the diamond that filled the clay body of the little elephant, she herself knew it existed. She was tremendously concerned, too, about Paul and Eleanor and, as she looked at him now, about Wythe.

This wasn't the self-sufficient man she had met—ages ago, it seemed. He was older than she had thought at first and tired and uneasier than he wanted her to know.

His body sagged in the deep chair. Though he sat, elbow on chair arm, chin on palm, his face almost hidden, she could see his eyes. They were strained with concentration.

He lifted his head and looked at her, then smiled.

"The mastermind has an idea. Several of them, in fact. One is, there is some way of getting in and out of the Fabrica we don't know about. The second is—your Unprotecting Arm. I won't use it all, but I must have at least a link from that little chain."

Reluctantly she removed the scarfpin, detached the arm, and gave it to him. He put it carefully away in a pocket.

"Now, the third thing—those books."

"You'll have to get them then. They're beyond my reach."

He followed her toward the reception hall but, when she put her hand on a light switch, stopped her.

"Wait a moment. Do you know your way round here in the dark? If you don't I do." As he spoke he moved round the living room, dimming all the lamps but one.

"I think I do. Why?"

"We don't know where Mukerji is."

"You don't think he's anywhere about! Baroneza would never sleep like that if he were."

"No, I don't think he's in the house. Come on."

They moved cautiously over the highly waxed floor of the reception sola to Penny's room. The high windows, two on the north, four on the west, framed dark masses of mango trees and shrubs outside, a sky brilliant with stars, made darker and more brilliant still by the heavy screens and bars. In the enormous room the furniture loomed black except where three mirrors were luminous.

"Let's get the shades down," Wythe suggested, and, keeping in the shadow, they did.

In the bathroom he lifted down the bulky package of books and looked up at the high windows above their heads. "I guess this is as good a spot as any to go over them. This house is alive with doors and windows."

Sitting on the tiled floor with the lamp of the dressing table between them, whispering like two conspirators, they went through the books. After they opened the package, that is.

Brazil takes deep interest in all printed matter that enters its boundaries. Customs inspectors may be casual about examining incoming bags, but they do a thorough job on books and magazines. The official who had examined Penny's books, after passing them, had had them neatly and almost irrevocably tied up again.

Wythe and Penny skimmed through them swiftly, looking for notes or writing inserted in them. Nothing.

"How many did you have?" he asked.

"Seventeen."

He counted quickly. "Seventeen it is." They went through each one again, carefully, page by page. Nothing.

"Get the wrappers off and we'll take a look at the bindings."

Wythe was ripping off jackets as he spoke. Penny, following his example, gasped, "Look!"

The jacket she held out in one hand was new and shining, gay with title and design of a light summer novel. The book in her other hand, though giving small evidence of use, had obviously stood on the shelves of the SS *Paraguay's* library. On the inside front cover, concealed by the flap of the jacket, was the legend, "Property of the SS *Paraguay;* please return to Library."

Wythe seized it and started through it again. Penny sat quiet, a startled look in her shadowed eyes. The book was a biography of Fouché, by Stefan Zweig! When he turned to her questioningly she began to replace the jackets on the remaining books, now and then setting one aside.

"What are those for?"

"Dr. Attilio. I told him he could see them, and these seem to be the best—" she stopped. "What's the matter?"

"Did you offer them to him or did he ask to see them?"

"He asked. Why? We were just talking about books."

"Nothing." Wythe hesitated. "Just one of those silly questions one asks," he added wearily. "I can't see anything out of the ordinary about this *Fouché*."

They looked at one another. She was tired. But he was neither so tired nor—for once—so polite.

"Water and sleep are indicated. How about getting some while I go over this opus again? If something's here I've missed it."

"Not—not without me," she protested with more energy than she felt. Then she sat up suddenly, not tired at all. "What about the gateman? Was he to come back here or go straight to Mart?"

Before she finished he was on his feet, pulling her up. "Come on. He mustn't go to Mart."

He hadn't. He was waiting on the veranda, too scared to move. With the light in the living room dim and no sign of Wythe or Penny to answer his clapping, his poor old brain had simply stood still. He didn't know what to do next, so he had stood still too.

They brought him into the living room and closed the doors. His eyes, the whites, brown-stained and moist about dark pupils, were rolling in his deeply grooved black face. His arms beneath the old cape gestured helplessly. A battered hat trembled in one hand.

Nothing had been seen of Mukerji, he told Wythe in his jumbled Portuguese. The watchmen had come and gone on their rounds as usual. If Wythe said so, he'd go to Senhor Mart, but in the meantime, so that the morning gateman would not ask questions, he had checked Mukerji on his records as leaving at nine-fifteen.

"Espere um momento," Wythe told him. "Wait."

Turning to Penny, he translated, mumbled, then asked, "Can you bear this fragrant old rascal here for a few minutes more? I'd like to ask him some questions—about last night, for example."

Penny nodded and sank into a chair. She watched while little by little the old man wavered, then confessed whatever it was he had held back earlier in the evening.

Watched, too, when the ordeal was over, his confidence restored and his smiles and assurances of undying something or other as Wythe pressed money in his hand and saw him out the doors.

Wythe locked them securely before he crossed the room to look down at Penny with the greatest composure.

"Good news?" she asked hopefully.

"Hardly. But I think we've both passed the point where anything can surprise us now. At least I have. I've often wondered what my saturation point was. Tonight I think I know. One murder, another man missing, possibly a private spy or two, secret messages, and now the police on our trail. That does nicely."

"Police!" Penny's thoughts flew to her rescuer of the afternoon. "What did Haile tell you?"

"I won't repeat all he said, but the sense of it was this. A man did enter the grounds by the north gate last night—shortly after nine-thirty. He never went out. And who do you think he was?"

Wythe broke off then to admit, "I can't answer that question myself. But either the man you saw lying on the steps Wednesday night or the man who—as you think—murdered him was from the police or detective service. He flashed some sort of badge."

Before Penny's alarm his tone modified. "The thing that impresses me is this. Someone entered the north gate

last night, someone important enough to make him risk
his job by not reporting it. That clears the air a little.

"Two men came into the grounds last night. One, you
saw. The other, we'll say, is responsible for what you saw.
One came in by the north gate. How the other got in we
don't know. Both came for the same thing. At least one
came for something and the other obviously didn't want
him to get it."

Wythe stopped again, after a moment threw up his
hands. "I thought I was going to arrive somewhere when
I started that masterminding, but now it's all as clear as
mud. You go to bed, but give me that *Fouché* first. I'm
going to put it under Paul's pillows and sleep on it. Maybe his or my unconscious can make something of it. I'm
signing off."

Penny left him before his unconscious could make
something of the thought in her mind. Mart, of course,
could come and go at will, day or night, without using the
north gate. But Mr. Cochrane, surely, could also come and
go as he would. And Dr. Attilio—why not? And Paul—if
he were here!

Her thinking carried her to one of her north windows
with one more name in her mind. Wythe's. She had watched
him in the living room. And she had had to accept what
Wythe told her of what had been said in Portuguese!

Suddenly she pressed close to the window to peer at the
Casa gates. They were closed, but outside them someone
was carefully using a small flash. As she watched its light
turned upward for one brief instant. In that instant she
recognized the bright red thatch of Mart.

12

Delfina woke Penny the next morning. "Get up, Miss Penny. Mr. Cochrane is here."

Penny sat up quickly. "Mr. Cochrane! What time is it?"

"Almost eleven. He wants to talk to you. Then he is going to take you back to Rio for luncheon and the afternoon with his wife, he says." Delfina's voice dropped. "But you can't go, Miss Penny. Dr. Wythe wants you to come to his office at two o'clock."

From the door Delfina added, "And Dr. Wythe said he was taking a book of yours to finish."

Penny showered and slipped into slacks. As she appeared in the living room Delfina, breakfast tray in hand, led the way to the veranda. There Mr. Cochrane rose to greet her.

"I'm sorry to wake you, Penny. But I had to visit the factories this morning, so stopped in to see how you are. We won't disturb you if you wish to be quiet, but both Madge and I want you to feel our home is yours."

"Will you have coffee or a drink—while I eat breakfast?" Penny asked.

"No, nothing for me. I really came to talk with you seriously, Penny."

She put down her coffee cup and resignedly took up a cigarette. He hastened to light it.

"Now, all set? I want to ask you a straight question and I want a straight answer. Why did Paul dash off without even a moment's notice?"

She shook her head slowly. "I'm afraid I can't tell you, Mr. Cochrane. They were gone when I woke up."

"But didn't they leave a note of some kind—any message?"

"Just a line to say they would soon be back."

Mr. Cochrane waved that away too. "I expected you to say that. Now let's consider the preliminaries over."

Astonished at the change in his voice, Penny looked up. Mr. Cochrane was no longer the bland and paternal friend. His face was set and stern. Now he was much more understandable as the president of an American corporation in Brazil, she thought. But he gave her no time to think.

"As president of the U.E. in Brazil, I am responsible for Fabrica da Luz as well as the city offices. Paul is an excellent executive as well is one of the best glassmen anywhere. Then why, suddenly, like a heedless child, should he leave everything at loose ends?"

Penny looked at him squarely. "I can't believe Paul did, Mr. Cochrane. Dr. Attilio, Dr. Sloane, Mart, all the men I've met here are like the executives Paul had working with him in India—perfectly capable."

"Yes, yes, of course. That's not the point. This is the point, since you insist on evading it. I—we all spent the evening here Tuesday night. Up to midnight, it was evident, Paul had no thought of flying to New York. Yet he left at dawn. What did you tell him that changed his mind?"

When Penny did not answer he altered his tone. "I'm going too fast, but I see you understand me."

"I know nothing of business management, Mr. Cochrane, but I know Paul. It's too bad he didn't have time to talk with you, but I'm sure the first thing he'll do in New York, if necessary, is to make a satisfactory—"

His china-blue eyes were keen on her now. "I'm sure Paul left because of some very sufficient reason. But I do not believe his going had anything to do with the U.E." He waved that aside too. "Suppose we talk for a moment about you. Why are you here, for example?"

He paused to look at her skeptically. "After all, this is U.E. property. You have no connection with the U.E.—except as a guest of Paul and Eleanor."

Color crept into Penny's cheeks, but she remained silent until she could smile at him. She knew that technique. Pepperpot used it frequently to make her and others so angry they would speak without thought. "If you will give me half an hour I can move to a hotel."

Mr. Cochrane leaned back and laughed with pleasure. "Naturally not. I admire courage and loyalty in a woman, Penny. That's really what I wanted to know—that you could be trusted not to talk or lose your head. I know why Paul went to New York."

He rose then and held out his hand. "How about returning to Rio with me in an hour? Madge is looking forward to knowing you better."

"Not today, thank you. I'm simply awfully tired."

"Too tired to walk to the back gates with me?" His glance indicated the living room where Delfina could be seen and heard cleaning.

He paced beside her thoughtfully until they were out of range of the Casa. Then he turned with concern. "Take my advice, my dear, and be careful. More people than I believe you brought Satan's Sixth Finger to Dr. Attilio."

"How you talk!" Penny laughed. "How could I bring something that may not even exist?"

"Don't laugh," he warned sharply. "And don't be too clever. Dr. Attilio tried to be and revealed that the diamond had reached his hands. You tried to be and confirmed my information that Jay is in New York."

His amusement at her surprise was the equivalent of a chuck under the chin. "Ah, at last we find something to trade. If I tell you where Jay is, will you give me that message sent by Dr. Rosario to Dr. Attilio?"

Her eyes became alert. His expression changed to surprise, touched with chagrin.

"It was you, Mr. Cochrane, not the customs, who went through my things. You had them!"

"Of course," he admitted after a moment, his voice bland again. "I won't tell you how or why I knew to search your bags, but I certainly went through everything but your books. The customs had practically sealed them."

He stopped at the gates and put a hand on her arm. "Listen, my child. Paul is my best man in Brazil, and Dr. Attilio is his best man here. Do you think that when I see them walking blindly into a million-dollar-diamond scandal—yes, that's the word—I have no interest in saving the reputation of the U.E. as well as theirs and mine?

"You're my last straw—a charming one and not fragile, I'm glad to discover. Perhaps you don't know you have that message. But sooner or later you'll find it. You must have it. And let me make this clear. When you do find it bring it to me. To no one else. If you don't, I can't be responsible for anything that might happen."

He pressed her arm gently, turned, and went his way down the back road.

Walking thoughtfully back to the house, Penny encountered Delfina on the kitchen terrace, hanging rugs to sun on the railing. Again her expression baffled Penny, and she paused expectantly. When Delfina, however, seized a brush and prepared for action she went on into the house.

As she entered the living room the telephone rang. For the first time since her arrival she answered it.

"I wish to speak with my husband, Miss Paget," Madge Cochrane's thin voice shrilled in her ear.

"Oh, I'm sorry, Mrs. Cochrane. You can reach him at the lamp factory in a minute or two."

"He is there beside you now as he was yesterday, as he has been every day—"

Listening in amazement to the furious flow of words pouring over the wire, Penny felt the receiver abruptly leave her hand. Delfina, angry, too, replaced it with a bang in its cradle.

"I wish I had fleas," was her fervent comment.

Penny choked back her laughter. "What would you do with fleas?"

"Put them in her ears. Mr. Paul says that's the best thing to do when somebody wants to make trouble."

"She has called before? She believes Mr. Cochrane comes here?"

"She calls every day. Sometimes many times. You must not answer the telephone, Miss Penny."

As swiftly and silently as she had come, Delfina returned to her rugs, leaving Penny to gaze at the telephone with unbelieving eyes.

Shortly after two o'clock Penny again approached the brown varnished doors of Wythe's office. This time they stood open, and Wythe himself was waiting in the sunshine there for her.

Not the same man who had risen so politely to greet her just twenty-four hours before. Though something of the reserve had gone from his manner, gravity weighted his smile and greeting.

Yet as they stood in the doorway a moment, looking out across the Fabrica wall to the little hills in the valley, her experiences in Rio seemed like some fantastic story read long ago.

New little houses, stuccoed in fresh pastel shades, dotting the hills everywhere, might have been gardens of giant flowers against the green of the slopes. A long white wall running across the top of one a half mile or more away looked for all the world like a great white crown resting on a soft velvet cushion.

"Dr. Attilio's home," Wythe told her, following her glance.

They entered the office then, and Wythe closed the doors securely behind them. The order and quiet there were similarly out of key with the thoughts in their minds.

Through the open doors to the laboratories she looked into an intricate but organized maze. Over the white walls, the gray tables and cabinets sunlight from high windows danced and sparkled among racks of test tubes, rows of reagent bottles, and various glass containers. Three young Brazilian men moved about at work there. Somewhere the secretary tapped on a machine.

Wythe closed those doors also and, placing a chair for Penny beside his desk, stood waiting. "No one will disturb us now," he said.

With tightening nerves she took the chair to listen. But he was in no hurry to begin.

"How much do you know about chemistry?" he asked finally.

The lightness of his tone was not real, but she took her cue from him. "I know two parts of oxygen and one of hydrogen, or the other way round, form water."

He turned from her abruptly. Pushing some papers aside, he looked at two rough little chunks of glass lying side by side on his desk. One was the same bit he had tumbled from hand to hand as he listened to her story on Thursday. The other was somewhat larger.

Now he did not tumble either of them in his hands. He did not even touch them. He sat looking at them with so intent, almost solemn a gaze, for so long, that the fearful anticipation lying tense in Penny turned to wonder.

She had not seen this Wythe before. Here was a man of more emotional depth and sensitivity than she had realized. Watching him, her interest quickened in the man instead of what she had come to hear. What else lay behind the curtains in his guarded eyes, behind his smooth, controlled face, she was thinking when his finger, tapping the desk lightly before the smaller bit of glass, recalled her.

"Do you remember this? If I had known its story yesterday and this one's"—indicating the larger piece—"a lot of things might be different today."

"They're just blobs of glass, aren't they?"

"Just blobs of glass," he repeated. "But if I could be sure that by destroying them and persuading you to go back to New York—"

"What then?" she prompted, while her own thoughts returned to all that had happened in New York of which he was unaware.

"That we could end this ghoulish business."

"We? You aren't involved except through me."

He gave her an odd veiled glance. "You saw a man lying on the Casa steps Wednesday night. You *think* he was dead—murdered. I *know* a man was killed on the Fabrica property Wednesday night."

He looked from one to the other of the pieces of glass, then drew from an envelope near them her Unprotecting Arm and placed it between them.

"The whole story is there for anyone who can read it. I haven't read it all yet."

As she struggled to understand his thought Penny drew a deep breath. This new Wythe, his voice deep with feeling, with something else she couldn't grasp, exerted a curious force over her. He attracted her strongly, yet somehow, too, appeared to keep her away.

"If it's something so—so dreadful, Wythe, why don't we? Destroy the glass, I mean."

"It's too late. Whatever is behind this hasn't just begun. We can't stop it."

"Then let it go on without us!" she cried. "Let's get out of it right now! I'm—I'm really frightened—"

"Of what?" he asked quickly. "For what?"

"Of what you say. For both of us. You may be next—or I!"

Again that glance. "Have I frightened you so much? Or has something else happened?"

"I don't know—really. Perhaps it's just that so many things—one after the other—have happened. Mr. Cochrane came to the Casa this morning. He knows about the diamond. He knows why Paul went to New York. And he believes I brought a message—"

Wythe whistled. "So Cock is around playing the big, bad wolf. Interesting. Very."

He leaned forward unexpectedly and tilted her chin with a finger. "You're here." He smiled. "The diamond's here. And so are these." He nodded at the bits of glass and Unprotecting Arm. "This isn't going to be easy to give or to take," he warned. "I'll make it as simple and short as I can. But if I'm not clear or if I omit anything you want to know, stop me and ask. Promise? The place we're coming out is so far removed from everyday experience you must know every step of the way back."

13

Wythe picked up two large empty electric bulbs from a tray on his desk and looked down at one of them a moment before passing it to Penny.

"We make two kinds of glass here in Fabrica da Luz—lead glass and lime glass. At present we are making only lead glass. We supply all the lamps used on Rio's streets. Now we are busy on a huge rush order for them. They are made of lead glass.

"That one you are holding in your hand is made of lead glass. It came from one of four pots in our Number Two Furnace. It was made on Wednesday."

At her vague glance he smiled. "I'll take you over later to the glass factory and show you the furnaces and how glass is made and a lamp blown. But perhaps you can understand this now.

"We have three furnaces in the glass factory. Each furnace contains eight pots. In these pots the mixture for making glass is placed like—like pouring sugar into eight sugar bowls. The only difference is that all eight pots in one furnace are seldom filled with a new mixture at one time.

"Tuesday—the day you arrived in Rio—four of the eight pots in Number Two Furnace were filled at the same time with the same mixture. That means all were subject to the same heat and a lot of other things you don't need to know about for the melting process.

"Wednesday morning those four pots were opened and perfect glass bulbs—like that one in your hand—were made from all of them. The pots were closed up Wednesday night and opened again Thursday morning.

"Thursday morning the same glass blowers who worked the pots on Wednesday made perfect lead-glass bulbs from three of them."

"Three?" Penny asked to show she was following him intelligently.

"Three." He touched the lamp in her hand. "That's a perfect lamp. The end is round, the glass clear. Hold it up to the light."

She did. Except for its larger size, it was exactly like the bulbs she used in her New York apartment.

"Now look at this one." He gave her the second shell. "See any difference?"

"Of course."

The end of the second shell was flat, like the bottom of a flash, and had a large irregular dent in it. And when she held it against the light she could see little specks or bubbles in the neck.

"That particular shell has nothing to do with what I'm saying except as illustration," he told her. "It was made some time ago. But its irregular shape and the cords or seeds—you called them specks and bubbles—will show you what I mean. Now take a deep breath.

"That shell in your hand is made of lime glass. Lime glass requires more heat than lead glass to melt it and to make it sufficiently fluid to be blown into the shape of a lamp.

"When a lime-glass mixture is melted, therefore, in a furnace regulated for a lead-glass mixture the glass is too thick, too stiff, to be blown properly. The glass blowers have great difficulty in handling it. Frequently they don't have breath enough to blow the glass evenly down to the bottom of the mold.

"That flattened and concave dent you see in this lamp shell is a frequent result. But dents can appear in one side or the other. Now is all that clear so far?"

Penny nodded as she gave the shell back to him. Inwardly she was wondering what a lecture on glassmaking had to do with a man murdered on the Casa steps.

But Wythe's finger was tapping the desk again before the smaller chunk of glass.

"Thursday morning Orlando—one of my laboratory boys—went out on his regular round of the glass factory to bring back samples of glass from each pot in the three furnaces. It's part of our routine to check those samples every day as soon as they come in.

"The foremen for furnaces one and three each gave him eight samples. The foreman of Number Two Furnace gave him seven. When Orlando asked for the eighth the foreman told him Pot Seven had been closed for the day, that something was wrong with the mixture.

"My boys are keen to learn everything possible about glassmaking in Brazil, so Orlando asked for a sample from Pot Seven anyway. The foreman picked up this piece from the floor and gave it to him. See?"

Wythe turned the sample about before Penny carefully. "It's just a rough fragment of glass. Nothing unusual about it, except it appears very wavy and a little milky."

He looked at it himself for a long moment before he went on.

"Orlando brought this sample to me when he returned and told me what had happened. Suspecting that some foreign material might have been thrown into the glass mixture, I told him to ask my analyst to test it for calcium

and excess aluminum. We are very busy these days, and
that was a neat short cut.

"Just a minute or two before you arrived yesterday Dr.
Assis, my analyst, brought me back this sample of glass
and his analysis of it.

"He found in the glass a rather low percentage of aluminum but a high percentage of calcium and phosphorus.
Calcium and phosphorus as well as aluminum are apt to
produce wavy glass, and phosphorus will also cause that
milkiness I showed you.

"While you were telling me about your experience on
Wednesday night my mind kept going back to what Dr.
Assis had reported. I was wondering why Pots Five, Six,
Seven, and Eight in Number Two Furnace could all have
contained good lead glass on Wednesday but only Pots
Five, Six, and Eight contain it on Thursday.

"I suppose that was why I picked up the piece of glass
and played with it while I listened to you. 'What happened in Pot Seven Wednesday night?' I kept asking myself. Where could calcium and phosphorus come from?

"But after you left I thought of you and what you had
told me. Your story kept getting in the way of my thinking
about this glass sample from Pot Seven. First, I'd think
about the glass and then about something you'd said until in a curious sort of way the two problems—shall I call
them?—were blended together.

"An explanation for the calcium and phosphorus in the
glass sample popped into my mind but was too incredible
to accept. I went over Dr. Assis' analysis again and wasn't
satisfied with it. So I sent Orlando back for a second and
larger sample from Pot Seven. This is it."

Wythe picked up the larger lump of glass and placed it
near her. "You'd better look at it."

Penny took it uncertainly. She couldn't see where this
long explanation was heading, but from the seriousness

and care with which Wythe selected each word she was beginning to feel again that same tingle of terror she had known on the Casa veranda Wednesday night.

"It—it looks just like the other piece," she heard herself saying in a voice unlike her own. Thin and brittle, it came from the top of her throat.

"Does it? Are you sure?"

She turned it round again. "Well—except for this." She touched a tiny hole of yellowish-brown color, about the size of a pinhead. From it blurred streaks of brilliant red ran out like rays.

"I saw that too," he agreed significantly. Taking the sample back, he placed it carefully beside the other.

"We tested this second piece of glass late yesterday afternoon," he went on slowly. "It, too, contained calcium and phosphorus. No doubt about it. And then when my boys went home at five I tested this little spot of red. Perhaps you can see where I chipped some of it away?

"Two things are commonly used to make glass red. One is selenium. The other is gold. As we have selenium here in the factory, I tested for that first, naturally. Selenium, however, did not stain that glass. So I tested for gold. And gold it was—is."

Something was struggling to click in Penny's mind.

Wythe gave her no time to concentrate on it.

"From the time I finished those tests until I went up to see you at eight-thirty or so I sat at this desk thinking about them. No, as Delfina no doubt told you, that isn't all I did. I wore out the wires calling her about you. I was in a state of mind by that time about your going outside the grounds alone.

"But I still wasn't willing to admit what my tests were telling me. And when Delfina finally telephoned to say you were back I kept putting off the moment of going up to see you. I wasn't eager to. I didn't know how to tell you what I'm telling you now. Or how you would take it."

"You aren't eager to tell me now, are you?" she asked. "And why didn't you tell me last night?"

"Your Unprotecting Arm—of gold and silver—for one thing. As soon as I saw it was not a real *figa* I decided to make another test. To make it this morning and to tell you the results of all my tests in my office—when the sun would be shining and the setting more—more realistic."

"And now?"

"You don't know? You haven't understood?"

Penny looked away from his searching eyes. One part of her mind was numb with horror. The rest would not believe what her ears had heard. She shook her head.

"Calcium may come from a number of different sources," Wythe began again, watching her keenly. "A tile, a chunk of cement, a brick, a piece of pottery or marble. Any one of them dropped into a glass mixture would produce it.

"But it seemed unlikely these would melt completely at the usual furnace temperatures. Or that a sufficient quantity of any one of them to produce the high percentage of calcium Dr. Assis found would be thrown into a pot.

"It seemed still less likely that the common variety of such articles to be found around a factory or in this section of the city, would contain gold. In the light of what you told me, it occurred to me that one other thing could do it."

Penny's eyes, wide and fearful on his, asked the question.

"Yes. The body of a man."

His eyes searched her face again before he added, "Calcium and phosphorus are the essentials of the ashes of a man's body."

14

When Penny said nothing Wythe's face cleared. But inside her something leaped as if a shock of cold electricity had been released. It ran over her in icy waves to focus about her throat.

"After you left yesterday I suspected the truth," he went on then. "But I couldn't—perhaps wouldn't—believe it. The analysis of the second sample, however, proved that a man—a man, mind you—had been murdered here. And when this morning I tested a link of the broken chain on your Unprotecting Arm—"

He stopped, said abruptly, "I have one more test to make. It will take longer."

"Why? Isn't this—enough?"

"No. You saw a body lying on the Casa steps Wednesday night. Near those steps you found this little arm. I know a man's body was destroyed in Pot Seven Wednesday night and that with it was destroyed some sort of gold ring or rings. This final test will prove whether the man you saw and the man whose body was placed in Pot Seven were the same man or two different men."

Penny remained still. Wythe swung round in his chair to look up at the high window above him. Its light revealed how pale his own face had become. After a few minutes he swung back, looking at his watch.

"It's after three, Penny. If you can take any more we'll go over to the glass factory and I'll show you exactly what happened." He smiled a little. "After all, you started this. Now we've got to see it through. And I've already asked Dr. Attilio if I could show you around."

"I—I want to know," Penny told him. "Somehow I feel better now. Knowing is much easier than suspecting, imagining—being afraid."

"O.K. then. Let's go." Wythe rose. "But remember, you're just a visitor in Rio, seeing the sights of the big city."

Leaving the little path to the office doors, they turned left on the pavement and passed a series of warehouses where men were loading trucks with cartons of lamps. Soon they entered the shadowed section of the factories where flamboyant trees arched on both sides. Here the glass and lamp factories stood well back from the road on a raised stone-banked terrace.

As the first floor of the glass factory was given over to the checkerwork of the three great furnaces and storage space, he led her up an outside stairway directly to the floor where the lamps were blown.

They stopped in the entrance of a dim and vast room while Wythe looked about for Dr. Attilio. He was not difficult to identify. His large, dignified figure loomed above men in the simplest working clothes, working in groups down the long floor. Dr. Attilio was exceptionally well groomed, even to a tiny purple orchid in his lapel.

"This is a pleasure, Miss Penny," he said, hurrying forward. "You are enjoying Rio?"

"I'm thrilled with what I've seen so far."

"Perhaps you see us with a visitor's eyes. Most foreigners find much to be improved here. Especially North Americans. They are expert improvers—and very good for Brazil."

Wythe, beside Penny, moved suddenly, and Dr. Attilio smiled. "Here's another work-bound North American, impatient to return to his laboratories to improve Brazilian glass. Shall we send him back? It will give me great pleasure to show you. . . ."

"Not at all, Dr. Attilio," Wythe assured him. "I've told Penny how busy you are. Besides," he added, taking her arm to draw her away, "your expert knowledge would be wasted on her. My explanations will do very well."

Dr. Attilio laughed and stepped back. "I'm sure he misjudges you, Miss Penny. If you think so, too, come back to me—any time."

"Thank you, Dr. Attilio. And my books are ready for you any time." When they were safely down the floor she turned to Wythe.

"Don't say it," he apologized. "I had to get rid of him. 'Expert knowledge'—nice touch."

"I understood that. I was about to admire his English. It's a lot better than yours or mine."

"Most Brazilians in high places speak English and French, German or Italian. They have a gift for languages. Look at Delfina. You can't use a word today she won't be tossing around tomorrow."

They were passing Number One Furnace, or rather the top of it. The base ran down through the first floor into the ground. Set into this igloolike dome, shoulder to shoulder, around its complete circumference were eight fat cream-colored pots. Round mouths open, molten glass radiant at different levels in their interiors, they shriveled Penny with their hot breath.

Around the furnace on tiny podiums were the glass blowers. Some stood firmly and with a lovely grace, holding their blowpipes to their lips to trumpet soundlessly like so many incognito Gabriels. Others swung their pipes in rhythmic arcs, the tips of red-hot glass weaving patterns of light in the dimness.

Still others were inserting pipes into iron molds at their feet to round out the glass pendants into finished shells. A few, while exchanging empty pipes for fresh ones apprentices supplied, took time to inspect Wythe and his guest.

Two more furnaces similarly busy ranged down the floor. And far beyond them, stacked in rectangular pyramids on floor and wooden tables, were assortments of lamp globes. Sunlight from open windows at the end of the room illumined their translucent blues, greens, grays, rose. Here and there like banks of fresh snow were the huge white globes used in Rio's streets.

Wythe stopped her beside the second furnace. "Can you look as if I were explaining this just for your casual interest?" he asked. And while he said one thing with his hands for the eyes of others, he said another for her ears.

"We're now in front of Number Two Furnace. Notice anything about its position? No, don't look round; I'll tell you. It stands between those offices for recording machines and what not behind us and that area of plain wall across from us. Back and front they shut this furnace off from outside observation. No silhouette or movement here could be seen from the outside by the night watchmen.

"Theoretically all night long a watchman should go round this floor every hour. Actually he slips himself a cigarette in the back room or, if he is really conscientious, strolls around Number One Furnace. Anyone near Number Two would have plenty of time to get out of sight when he heard a watchman coming up that stairway we climbed.

"There's another stairway on the back of the building. But it isn't lighted at night and the watchmen don't use it. Its door opens just behind us, beside that last little office. Now it's closed to prevent drafts.

"That's the stairway the—the murderer, I think, used or would have if he knew this factory, and it appears he did. Luck was with him and against him, too, because two firemen are always on duty at night here. They keep the fires regulated.

"From shortly after ten o'clock Wednesday night they were busy cleaning the grates downstairs. I checked that first thing. The noise they make would cover any sounds up here."

"What was the bad luck then?" Penny interrupted.

"That the firemen *were* downstairs. I think the body was brought here to be thrown on the powerful fire of one of the grates. That would have been much simpler."

"Simpler?"

"Yes, and less dangerous. I'll explain in a minute."

Wythe drew her round a step to stand directly in front of a pot.

"That is Pot Seven. Five and Six are on our left. Eight, on our right. This man near me is Tonico, one of our best glass blowers."

He smiled up at the worker who, aware that Wythe was talking about him, made some extra flourishes with his pipe.

"Tonico usually works a pot alone. On Wednesday he had Pot Seven. Therefore, it's safe to say when he knocked off for the day the pot was left about half full.

"He had Pot Seven again on Thursday morning. When he found the mixture stiff, making shells like that one with the dent in it I showed you, he reported to the foreman. And, when Dr. Attilio arrived on the dot of eight-thirty, as he has every morning since this factory went up, the foreman reported Tonico's complaint. Dr. Attilio ordered the pot closed."

Wythe hesitated, then went on steadily.

"A man's body, especially a small man's, could be placed in a pot. If it were—dismembered. On the grates below that wouldn't have been necessary. That's why I said the murderer was unlucky. He brought the body here to throw it on a fire and get away quickly. When he found the firemen there he had to do something else—and fast. He came up the back stairway. You see now?"

Penny nodded. "Go on."

"But when he got it here he found the pot mouths too small for his purpose. He must have—operated on the body—in the dark on the outside platform of the stairway. The rain removed all traces. I'm just guessing, but that seems logical. He certainly didn't do it in here."

Wythe stopped abruptly. "I wonder what he did with the clothes."

Penny moistened her heat-dried lips. "But wouldn't Tonico have noticed? I mean, wouldn't the level of the molten glass have been different—on Thursday morning? Higher?"

She was startled to hear her own voice asking the question, though it was in her mind. "Wouldn't he see—?"

"What could he see? Flesh would be consumed almost immediately at the temperatures of these furnaces. Any gases would be carried off rapidly through the openings between walls and roof. The skeleton would be reduced to a layer of loose bones floating on the surface of the red-hot glass. The bones would be slowly dissolved, leaving the mixture Tonico found Thursday morning. That is—a stiff and thick lime glass!"

Wythe looked at her questioningly. "I can go into details if you wish, but they're not—not pleasant. Besides, I want you to understand something else.

"A man's body, if put into one of these pots, wouldn't sink to the bottom of the mixture. It would float. So would any small pieces of metal on that body. The rest of the chain of that Unprotecting Arm, for example. But only for example, remember.

"Some small pieces of metal did go into this mixture. How many, I don't know. But I can't believe that second sample of glass from this pot could have registered the only one.

"You see, in the glass mixture there are, among other things, soda ash and niter. They act as a sort of spoon. They help to keep the mixture stirring during the melting and refining processes. Really, this stirring is due to gases they produce. They bubble up through the mixture in the same way that boiling water bubbles."

He paused again. "I'm afraid this is a very long explanation. Getting tired?"

"Awfully," Penny confessed. "But finish it—if all this is necessary."

"It is. Well, when this mixture is all melted and all the gases have been given off, the glass lies quiet, like stiff molasses. Then it's ready to be blown into shells. Into perfect shells or bulbs, that is. That was the kind of lead glass Tonico used all day Wednesday.

"When he started work on Thursday he naturally drew his glass from the top of Pot Seven, where the bones of the skeleton had been dissolved. As the mixture had not been stirred up by anything that would cause that surface layer of 'high lime' to be distributed through the rest of the mixture, the result was—the result was that poor Tonico tried to blow lead-glass lamps from lime glass!"

Wythe broke off. When his silence continued Penny turned to see his eyes narrowed on Pot Seven.

"What's the matter?"

"My two samples of glass came from the surface of that layer, too, of course," he answered, half to himself. "If the man who put that body there knew his chemistry he'd need only to take off the top layer to clear the mixture. Below it would be the original lead glass! I must think up some discreet questions for Orlando to ask the foreman of this furnace."

Again he was silent so long Penny became uneasy. The glass blowers were beginning to turn curious glances in their direction.

"What about the gold in that second sample?" she prompted. "How did it get into the pot if—if the clothes were taken away?"

"I don't know. It must have been on the body itself. The murderer either didn't see it in his haste and the darkness and rain or thought it too small to matter. This is the point about the gold. The physical properties of any metal put into a mixture like this would be destroyed. Their shapes, however, particularly if the pieces were small, would be retained."

At her puzzled glance he explained: "That is, a long thin piece would leave, more or less, a long thin line as an impression of its presence. A small round piece would leave a small round impression. And if the metal were gold it would leave its impression in color. That again is due to lack of stirring."

"And one of those tiny links on my Unprotecting Arm would leave that little round dot on the second sample! Oh, Wythe, let's go. I can't listen to any more!"

"Take a deep breath. You're all right. If we don't go round the rest of the floor Dr. Attilio will be out to show it to you. And don't jump to conclusions. I won't know for some time whether that dot in the second sample and those gold links on the Unprotecting Arm have anything in common."

He took her arm in a firm grasp and drew her away. "Come and look at this *lehr*—oven to you," he said in a clearer tone as two American men came down the floor with Dr. Attilio. "It takes three hours for those globes to travel from one end of that moving belt to the other. This is where they're annealed so they won't crack and drop on that long bob when you're walking along the streets."

So they moved slowly down the long—the endless—room and back to the doorway and down the stairs and out into the sunlight.

On the terrace at last, they dropped down on a bench beneath the mango tree. The sun was sinking through graying clouds to settle for the night in a nest of mountains. But neither sky nor mountains nor the delicately changing light held charms for them now.

Wythe, looking over Penny's head, whistled softly. "Don't turn round," he warned. "Mart's coming down the back road from the Casa—looking for you, perhaps. Listen; could you do a little expert work on that lad?"

"On Mart?"

"Why not? Oh, I know he's Paul's white-haired baby, but he isn't mine. And I've just thought of something. Mart's house may be the other entrance into the Fabrica we are looking for! Why didn't I think of that before? Our mysterious visitors could walk through his front door into his garden and enter by a little private gate."

"But the dogs. Delfina says they're really dangerous."

"Not with Mart around. Find out where he has been these past nights."

As Penny opened her lips to say where he had been last night, or rather early that morning, Wythe warned again, "Careful. Here he comes."

"So!" Mart's voice complained loudly behind them. "I now have to see before my very eyes—"

They jumped up and turned to find him glaring at them. "Move on. We cawn't have the uppah clawsses putting ideas into the heads of weary toilers. They'll pour out of those doors any minute now. Such goings on!"

"Count me in with the weary toilers," Wythe groaned. "And do something about cooling that glass factory. I've been showing Penny the sights and I don't think either of us will ever be the same again."

"Well, if you can make it to your laboratories alone I'll heave Penny up the hill. With Paul away, I have all the little grass roots up there to care for. Now is as good a time as any to look at them."

Without waiting for a reply he seized Penny's arm and turned her toward another of his short cuts.

"Let go of me, dynamite," he said as soon as they were beyond Wythe's hearing. "First you put on pretty slacks to seduce our worthy president. Now you flaunt that fetching costume to lead our intellectual chemist astray."

"So!" Penny mimicked. "You've been hanging over the gates again!"

"Again! What do you imply? Or is it infer?"

"That I saw you last night—this morning, I mean."

When he roared with laughter her rage rose again. "Stop that. It isn't funny."

"Funny? I think I'll just have the gardener run his lawn mower over that mop of yours and end all this. Paul left a note that if a hair of your head was harmed he'd have my neck when he returned. Well, when my dogs began to rage last night I rolled out to see what was up. Perhaps you think that's funny. A hard-working man tumbling out in the cold wintry dawn!"

He grinned at her, rather pretended to leer in a particularly horrible way. "Nothing was out of place except Dr. Sloane!"

When she refused to rise to that bait he continued, "The gate sheet showed he hadn't checked out. And though I didn't give a damn if he'd choked on some of his own brews in that untouchable laboratory of his, I know my duty. I investigate. And what do I find? His car outside.

No lights inside and no one either. Where could he be? Like a flash I know. Where would any ladybug be if he could? Shall I go on?"

"Skip to the slacks, please," Penny said hastily.

"My deep interest in Paul's grass roots took me to the Casa this morning—as soon as I thought you might have opened those lovely eyes. Too late again. You were already focusing them on our *presidente*. Learn anything?"

"You have a low mind, Mart. Mr. Cochrane was kind enough to stop in to see how I was—"

"Oh, I don't mean you could learn anything from him. Perish the thought! I mean was he able to penetrate the chilly granite of yon fair skull?"

Mart stepped in front of her. "I warned you once to keep away from that laboratory smoothie. Now I'm telling you to keep away from everyone. You have a good alibi—rest, quiet, sun are essential. Play it for all it's worth. Otherwise even a smart fellow like me can't keep you intact—till and if Paul returns."

Penny stepped round him to walk with head high to the gates. "Won't you come in?" she invited there with stony politeness.

Mart threw up his hands. "Spare me that."

"But the little grass roots," she reminded him. "You haven't seen them for as much as—fifteen minutes."

"Their green innocence is natural. And I can see from here they're doing all right. Just watch them and maybe you'll learn something. Almost anything would be a help. *Até logo.*"

He swung on his heel and strode back down the road. Excited barking inside the gates recalled Penny from her thoughtful observation of his receding back.

"No walk today," she apologized, slipping inside. "Oh, I'm such a fool, Baroness. I'm afraid. And I don't know who or what it is that frightens me."

To escape Delfina's eyes she walked round the house to the veranda and stretched out in a swing. Baroneza curled up beside her in a warm, comforting ball.

Where did Mart come into this? And why did he always appear at strategic moments? She could understand his antipathy for Wythe, Wythe's for him. But Mart seemed to have neither loyalty nor respect for anyone but Paul. And with a loyalty so strong—or at least vocal—would he permit anyone who had no business within the Fabrica walls to use his private gate?

Superintendent of grounds! That didn't require any particular technical experience, did it? Could Mart hold a position like that as a private eye for Paul? Paul had had such a man in India. The more she thought of it the more improbable it seemed that Mart would use his little gate against Paul's interests.

She smiled to herself. Paul would be amused to hear Mart's report that Wythe had spent a night in the Casa. Or would he? If Mart were his private eye he wouldn't be amused to know she had gone to Wythe when he'd told her to go to Mart.

Well, after this, she resolved, she wouldn't go to anyone. She'd keep her knowledge to herself and confine her attention to her own small affairs. The less she knew when this ghoulish thing, as Wythe called it, broke, the better it would be for all of them.

She was trying to remember all that Wythe had explained about glass manufacture, when Dr. Attilio appeared around the side of the Casa.

"See? I am a man of his word," he told her as he took her hand. "But first, you found interest in my factory?"

"Oh yes." She tried to inject enthusiasm into her eyes and voice. "Someone should paint your glass blowers—especially Tonico. He's as graceful as a dancer."

"So Tonico is what kept you so long beside Number Two Furnace!" Dr. Attilio was amused but pleased too. "And I thought it was my glass that absorbed you."

He seated himself beside the swing. "You are right. Someone should paint Tonico—and the others. Alas, their day will soon be done. With the new factory, lamps will be blown by machinery."

"Coffee? Something else to drink?" Penny asked.

He shook his head. "No, my dear young American. Unfortunately customs are different in my country. I must stay but a moment—just long enough to see your books."

Penny brought out the half dozen she had set aside for him. He picked them up, one at a time, glanced at their titles, and put them aside. "How beautifully you do books in America! And what beautiful prices we must pay for them here. I shall read all of these. But—you have more?"

"Those are the best."

"If you will, Miss Penny, let me see them all. You over-estimate my taste for English."

But when she brought out the rest he put them aside after a rapid inspection. "I admit defeat. These, no."

Impulsively Penny threw overboard Mart's warnings, her own recent decision to confine herself to her own affairs. "I have one more," she told him, watching through her lashes his face light up. "Dr. Sloane is reading it now. It's not a mystery, but there is a mystery about it."

"Yes?"

"On the voyage down someone entered my stateroom, searched my things several times. Once I saw who it was. A very gentle old man."

Dr. Attilio's face became still. "Perhaps," he suggested quietly, "your story amplifies mine—of Tuesday night?"

"Perhaps. That is why I thought to tell you, Dr. Attilio."

He rose. "Shall we talk in the house? It grows dark and will be cool here shortly."

When she rose, too, he spoke again softly. "But tell me now, Miss Penny. This book Dr. Sloane is reading—it is a biography of Fouché?"

Without waiting for her to answer in words he hurried to open the doors to the living room. "And now," he prompted as soon as they were seated. "You spoke of Barbados," she said hesitantly, "of a kinsman of yours—found dead there. I—I think he was on the ship with me."

"You will describe the gentle old man first, please."

As she added detail to detail of what she had observed about the first Dr. Rosario his face darkened, became set. "He was without doubt my kinsman—cousin—Dr. Rosario de Sousa." For an instant Dr. Attilio's long, flexible fingers quivered on the arm of his chair. "And the others— tell me quickly, Miss Penny."

He shook his head when she described Senhor Rodrigo. "So many Brazilians, Argentinians, Chileans"—he threw out his hands—"are medium height, slender, brown-skinned, black-haired. I do not recognize him."

"Before I describe the man who came aboard at Barbados I'll tell you what happened."

Rapidly Penny sketched her hours in the bay on B Deck and their arrival at Barbados. Dr, Attilio listened intently without interruption.

When she finished he spoke quietly, almost impersonally. "It was then Dr. Rosario sent me the wireless to say you had a message for me in *Fouché,* a book about which we had some correspondence when it was first published years ago. When you did not have your books here Tuesday evening I did not press the matter. I—I have Satan's Sixth Finger, thanks to you. Of that we will speak later, when the Olivers return."

He sat silent for a long minute. "I—for a time I have thought I would say no more—do no more about that message. My kinsman is dead. I did not know him well, have not seen him for many years. He was a diamond expert in Amsterdam. It is too late to help him now. And that message—"

Slowly he shook his head, rose. "No, I shall not speak of it to you. Let Dr. Sloane read the book. He can find nothing. And I—I think I do not want to know what that message says."

The telephone bell crashed into a silence Penny did not dare to break. She slipped hastily into the foyer and took up the receiver.

"This is the voice of the little grass roots," Mart informed her. "Get that bird out of there. In ten minutes I'm bringing up my dogs."

"Keep them where they belong. I'm busy."

"Well, half an hour, then. Not a moment longer." The connection broke off in her ear.

Dr. Attilio was still standing as she had left him. "You will tell me now about Barbados? What happened there?"

She told him rapidly. Every sound outside suggested the baying of Mart's savage dogs.

Dr. Attilio did not press her for details, but when she told of her discovery of the false Dr. Rosario he turned suddenly to stone. She felt as if she were talking into space or down a well. Not a glance or movement revealed his thoughts. When she finished he asked, "You have not repeated this story to anyone else?"

She shook her head.

"Good. You will not? For the present?"

"No," she promised. "Then you think I was right? There were two Dr. Rosarios?"

"There was only one Dr. Rosario," he corrected. "The other— But it is unthinkable that that man can have returned to this country!" His voice changed. "You have seen him again?"

"No. Only Senhor Rodrigo. On the Avenida Thursday afternoon."

"Miss Penny, I have changed my mind. I must have that *Fouché*. You can get it from Dr. Sloane—discreetly, of course? You will not mention my name?"

"If you don't need it tonight it should be simple. He'll probably finish it—"

"Good. I count on you." Dr. Attilio moved toward the door, turned back suddenly. "These men—Senhor Rodrigo and the—the other. They do not know you suspect?"

"I'm afraid they do know, Dr. Attilio. Senhor Rodrigo at least."

His face grew graver still, if that were possible. "Then it is important—for your own sake—to get that book for me."

"For mine?"

"Yes, Miss Penny. I can do nothing until I have that information. You are not safe here—alone. And we cannot go to the police—yet."

To his surprise Penny smiled and held up a hand. "Listen. Those are Mart's dogs. He's bringing them up to spend the night in the Casa grounds."

An answering smile flicked across Dr. Attilio's dark eyes. "In that case I need have no worries for you tonight. But Mart? Why does he do this? What does he know?"

Penny shook her head. "So far as I know, nothing at all. Paul asked him to keep me out of mischief."

"Paul knew before he left you would need such protection!"

"No, no. This is Mart's own idea."

"I wonder." Dr. Attilio stepped out on the veranda slowly. "Have you any reason to think, Miss Penny, that Paul did not go to New York? That he is in Rio?"

The sound of barking dogs grew louder. He did not wait for an answer but hurried down the steps and round the path to the Casa gates.

15

Stretched out in a lounge chair on the lawn late Saturday morning, Penny felt life still included some pleasant moments after all. In the gardens the mosquito men she had wanted to see ever since Wythe mentioned them were conveniently at hand. Two dark, short men in cotton khaki uniforms and black-visored khaki caps, they poked about, examining the pipes of the swimming pool and all the nooks and corners of the gardens where water might collect.

Finally they settled down to a detailed inspection of the lily pond. Occasionally as they peered and poked they turned curious glances on her. But that, she felt, was fair enough, for her own curious gaze never left them.

One of them soon departed, indicating with dramatic gestures that he would return. The other, seating himself on the pool's ledge, apparently fell asleep.

Perhaps Penny dozed herself. When she looked again the missing man had returned and was pouring minute fish from a battered pail into the pool. Two men in blue uniforms stood watching him.

Delfina, appearing to say her luncheon was served, eyed the newcomers with disfavor. The khaki-clad men, she explained on the way to the house, were *mata-mosquitos*— mosquito killers. They were outside men who came once a week to go over the grounds. The blue-uniformed men were *ajudantes,* a combination of inspector of the work of the outside men and, in their own right, inside men.

"What are they doing here so late on Saturday?" Delfina grumbled. "Now they'll poke into every corner of my clean house." As she served Penny she complained still more. "One of them is new. The senhora would call him a new broom. He's into everything with his flashlight."

But Penny, curious, hurried her luncheon to follow them round. They were looking into everything. They even flashed their lights into the water of the flower bowls and sniffed to make sure it was fresh. Their flashlights swept the floor boards and up the corners of each room to the ceilings, searched the top of wardrobes and cupboards, behind books in the bookcases. And, as Delfina had said, the new man was a veritable new broom. He exhausted even Penny's interest. She returned to her chair under the mango.

The *ajudantes* had hardly left by the back gates when Wythe strolled in the Casa gates. As he dropped down on the grass beside her he pulled *Fouché* out of his pocket.

"I've tested pages of this cursed book with every kind of dope I can think of for invisible writing. No luck. I'm afraid if any message is hidden in it it's in code, and that's beyond me. In books and movies underlined words or dots always give the mastermind a clue. There isn't a mark in this opus that I can see."

"Give it up," Penny suggested, holding out her hand for it.

"Mind if take it home over the week end? I'd like to read it. From pages I've skimmed it's interesting."

Penny opened her lips to protest. Thought better of it.

Delfina appeared as he spoke, bearing a tray with two tiny cups of coffee.

"Good for you, Delfina!" he exclaimed. "You think of everything, don't you?"

"I think something queer is happening," she declared darkly. "I bring the coffee as an excuse. Miss Penny, two more *ajudantes* are here to go through the house."

"Let them go," Wythe advised. "They come every week, don't they?"

"But two of them have just finished taking the house apart," Penny explained. "They left just before you arrived."

"That's not all," Delfina informed them. "Miss Penny, one of these new *ajudantes* is that fellow who was here Thursday night. I'm sure. He wears dark glasses—"

"Mukerji!"

"Where are they now?" Wythe asked.

"In the kitchen. I didn't tell them others were here this noon—"

"These chaps must have seen the yellow flag stuck in the north gate," Wythe suggested. "That means *mata-mosquitos* are inside. They probably figured since the mosquito killers had come so late—they don't work on Saturday afternoons—the *ajudantes* wouldn't be around until Monday. Let them go through the house, Delfina. Why not?"

"But why?" protested Penny. "It's been done once."

"Well, if one is Mukerji he might as well learn now that what he's looking for isn't here." Wythe touched his pocket carelessly. "Then perhaps he'll leave you alone."

"All right, Delfina, let them go," Penny said. "In a minute I'll come in."

A few minutes later she did go in, returning the coffee cups.

"They're in your room now," Delfina told her. "So are your sunglasses. You'll need them." She led the way to get them.

One man in a blue uniform was switching a flashlight up a corner of her bedroom wall. The other was not visible. Delfina, picking up Penny's sunglasses from her dressing table, rolled an eye toward the bathroom as she held them to the light.

"They're dusty. I'll wash them."

Penny followed her to see the second man on his knees before the shower booth, his head hidden by the tiled shower wall.

"Boa tarde," Penny said in her best and practically only Portuguese, strolling over.

The *ajudante's* head turned slightly and a muffled *"Boa tarde"* answered her. Then he leaned farther in to focus his flash on the drain in the corner. Nothing about him suggested her first and last English pupil, but she could recognize a narrow ear lobe when she saw it again.

Wythe looked thoughtful when she returned to her chair and verified Delfina's suspicions. "I was being nonchalant for Delfina's benefit," he said. "Look here, this means something—two sets of men, both in official uniforms. What were the first *mata-mosquitos* and *ajudantes* like, by the way?"

"Bona fide, apparently. Delfina knew them all— No, she didn't. One was new."

"You don't suppose the police are in this picture somewhere?" Wythe pulled up some blades of grass, sifted them through his fingers, threw them away. "Let's forget it. I came up to talk about something else. Don't you think you should have some young women friends here?"

Penny shook her head. "Let's wait a little. It's lovely out here and quiet, and I can use a lot of it now I'm used to it." Although Mart's warning—"If you won't promise to stay inside your own hedge I'll park these guardians here day and night"—rang in her ears, she nodded toward the mountains. "I love Brazil, don't you? I could never tire of those mountains."

"I'd give my life to be out of it!" The words evidently burst from Wythe of their own power, yet even the force behind them could not change the quiet level of his voice. He jumped up, took a step or two away, and returned.

"Do you know what I think I'll do? I've had my resignation written out for two months. I think I'll use this beautiful afternoon to present it to Cock."

"Wythe! You can't do that. At least wait for Paul—"

"Paul knows the laboratories are set up and functioning. That chemists to carry on the routine we're doing now are a dime a dozen. I think he wonders why I've stayed this long. There go your *ajudantes*. I'll follow their example—perhaps get a look at that Mukerji. *Até logo*. See you Monday."

But a few hours later, as Delfina was preparing dinner, Wythe telephoned. Penny learned then that something could make him raise the level of his voice.

"Is José there?" The words rang in her ears. "Drop everything and have him bring you here. I'll feed you. And bring Delfina too. We'll need her."

Antonietta, his colored maid, moving about a dining room off the foyer, was regarding them with undisguised interest.

"I got you up here to see the view really," he said to Penny. "The moon's almost full. And I lured Delfina under false pretenses too. Antonietta is leaving at eight for the country to stay with her son till Monday. I thought Delfina might help her out so that she can get away."

If his words were noncommittal, his eyes were not. They fairly shouted that something important had happened.

"Come, see my terrace," he invited when Delfina disappeared with Antonietta.

Once on the terrace Penny forgot him and his news. Above them curved the night sky, stars dimming before the rising moon. Below, all around, lay the city, a universe itself ablaze with millions of small suns. Between them and the harbor stretched a wide parkway, its winding marine drive arched with trees and aisled with lights.

To their left, guarded by a majestic row of palms, stood Gloria Church, solemn and dark. To their right, Gloria Hotel, bursting with light. Cars came and went before its doors, bringing Saturday-night diners. Beyond the marine drive, encircled by city and mountains, lay the harbor, the lights of Rio and of Niteroi pouring down and down into motionless waters. Behind everything rolled range on range, the ebony silhouettes of the Organs.

As she moved round the terrace to gaze at the radiant statue of Christ dominating the scene from the summit of Corcovado, the highest peak, Wythe came to stand beside her. "We're going to celebrate—"

"Don't tell me Mr. Cochrane accepted your resignation!"

His usually smooth forehead creased in a dark frown. "No. I found him in a bad moment. Something was eating him, and he took it out on me."

Terrace lights snapping on startled them. They turned round to see Antonietta approaching, cocktails and canapés on a tray.

"No, we're celebrating your first visit here," Wythe substituted.

As Antonietta disappeared he said significantly. "You may call it luck or coincidence, but I hope you'll call it deduction. That's what it was—partly."

"What was?"

"Wait. I must begin at the beginning. And the beginning is that I brought that book of yours home with me this afternoon. Going through it as often as I had, I'd read bits that made me want more. I stretched out on my couch downstairs and read till Chapter IV stopped me.

Me, personally, I mean. For it begins with one of the best essays on exile I've ever read. Or perhaps it only seemed so because I feel exiled down here and it meant something personal to me."

He laughed a little, embarrassed at revealing his feeling about it.

"Read it now," she urged as he drew the book from his pocket. Here was another Wythe and she was interested again.

"Oh, the essay isn't the point now. It's merely the medium. I'll just skim a few sentences to show you what started me on the road to discovery."

He switched on a light and, standing under it, read slowly, his voice tingling with excitement as he went on:

"Has anyone ever composed a hymn of exile? Has any poet ever sung the glory of this power that molds destinies, which uplifts those who have been cast down, which under the harsh stresses of loneliness reassembles in new order the dispersed energies of the soul? . . . The most notable messages have been delivered from exile. . . . Moses, Christ, Mohammed, Buddha, Luther, Dante, Nietzsche. . . . Even in the lower spheres of life, a temporary exclusion . . . gives a new freshness of vision. . . ."

Wythe closed the book and looked up. "That probably ruins the essay for you."

"No, it makes me wish I'd read the book on the boat coming down."

"I wish I'd read it sooner too. I didn't want to leave my work in New York. I was onto something big, but poor men can't choose. That's not important now. I didn't read further. In fact, I fell asleep, with the book open on my chest, thinking about that essay.

"When I woke up my living room was as black as night. Antonietta had come in and, seeing me asleep, had drawn the curtains. Not fully awake, I lay there thinking about the essay. It occurred to me that what exile had done for Moses, Buddha, and the rest had done for men in our own time—Hitler, Lenin, Stalin—was probably doing right now for men, voluntarily or not, in exile.

"That gave me an idea. Perhaps we were hearing from one of them now. Perhaps that little essay with its significant phrases was an arrow." Wythe passed the book to Penny, open at the essay. "Look at it."

She looked but could only see lines of black type on a white page.

"Keep on looking." He snapped off the terrace lights.

Under the pergola it was not as black as night, but it was dark. As Penny looked a faint glow began to develop on the page before her. Startled, she peered closely. The glow broke up into lines alternating with the black lines of type.

"What is it?" she demanded.

"I don't know." Wythe took the book from her and pushed it down securely in his pocket. "Some new trick ink possibly. But those lines of broken light you saw are words—Portuguese words. That's why I asked you to bring Delfina. We may need help."

"You haven't read it!"

"Just the first word or two. You started all this, you know. I thought you'd like me to wait till we could read it together."

A bell rang softly below as he spoke.

"I suppose we must go down." He rose reluctantly. "But that's what I saw when I picked up the book in the dark this afternoon. This is the message our friends are playing hide-and-seek to get."

16

Wythe in the dark dining room called off letter by letter the message written in light between the lines of the essay. Delfina, beside him, assisted occasionally. Sitting alone beside a reading lamp in the adjoining living room, Penny wrote each letter down.

The message was brief. When they reached the end they spread Penny's papers on the dining-room table. Wythe wrote out a condensed translation:

The stone is genuine—712.3 carats. Before cutting, value approximately $430,000. After, could attain one to one and a half million. Could be cut as one jewel but more practical to divide into fifteen or more. Much expert study needed to determine number and size of finished gems.

Penny and Wythe looked from the rough English words to one another, each with his own bewilderment. Delfina behind them uneasily eyed doors and windows.

"A million-dollar diamond!" Wythe paced a step or two, turned back to look at Penny oddly. "Did you know that—when you brought it down?"

Penny had sunk into a chair. Her face had lost all color.

Delfina came to her. "Come home, Miss Penny," she urged. Turning stern eyes on Wythe, she added, "You should burn those papers, Dr. Wythe. I don't know what they mean, but it isn't good."

"No. Perhaps not." He spoke gravely, but Penny felt his pleasure in having deciphered the message. Yet she could find no significance in it. Surely those facts and figures were nothing to alarm Dr. Attilio, interest Mr. Cochrane. Couldn't anyone who had the diamond get such information at any time? More important, she felt, was the necessity to get the book itself without rousing Wythe to questions and suspicions.

She wasn't going to get it, she realized, when she heard him speaking.

"If it weren't Saturday I'd take everything over to my bank," he was saying. "That's out, so I think we'll follow Delfina's advice and burn these papers, at least. The book is enough. And we don't want your handwriting mixed up in this, Penny. You burn these in something, Delfina. I'll take steps about the book."

While Delfina burned the papers one at a time in a metal tray Wythe did take steps. With a knife he carefully cut out the type block of the essay on exile, leaving the margins of the page as they were.

Penny watched attentively. His long fingers, accustomed to working with exactitude in his laboratories, moved precisely and without pause until the rectangle was removed. Then he took out his notebook to place it between the leaves.

"No. That won't do. The book remains to tell the tale."

He hurried into the living room, moving about there from bookshelves to tables, opening books and putting them down. At last a satisfied exclamation told them he had found what he wanted.

He returned with a book and laid it on the table beside *Fouché. Introduction to Argentina,* Penny read on its blue jacket.

"What has the Argentine to do with the message?" she asked as he hunted in a table drawer for something.

He came back with a roll of very narrow gummed tissue. "This," he told her, opening the books side by side. "*Fouché* and *Argentina* both have the same page size. Their type blocks are the same measure and kind. It will be a good trick if I can do it."

In the same way he had removed the type block from Fouché he removed a type block from the book on the Argentine. Then with infinitely careful fingers he reversed the blocks, inserting and gumming the essay on exile into *Introduction to Argentina* and the page from *Argentina* into *Fouché*.

"See if you can find it," he said when he had finished. Penny could, of course, because her fingers felt for the telltale tape. To anyone ignorant of the substitution, however, discovery would be difficult unless he read the two books through. Even then, reading in sun or lamplight, he could not have found the message *Introduction to Argentina* now contained.

Wythe placed *Fouché* on the little table beside the couch with other books he had been reading there. *Introduction to Argentina* he returned to its former place on a shelf.

"Really a mastermind," Penny applauded.

"They won't stand rough treatment, but they'll hold till Monday or till we can decide what to do next."

Penny's lips quirked at that "we."

"Shall we go up on the terrace to do it?" he suggested.

If he intended to tell her on the terrace what his ideas were he was defeated. For one reason because Delfina followed close on their heels, her determination not to be left alone with those books unmistakable. For another, the world appeared to have gone mad in their absence. Angry red moons were streaming across the sky, so many of them that the heavens seemed to be changing position.

"What's happening?" Penny cried.

Delfina laughed suddenly, an odd but welcome sound after the tension of the last two hours.

"Tonight is São João's Eve, Miss Penny. Those are balloons sent up by young men. They think if their balloon goes up safely it will reach São João—"

"Saint John," Wythe murmured.

"—in the sky and he will make the girl they want to marry say yes. If it falls, then they must wait another year. See? They are going up everywhere."

They were. From Niteroi across the harbor they mounted steadily to rush toward Rio on the night wind. From below and behind the apartment house balloons were climbing above the trees to speed away toward the mountains.

But many young men were doomed to disappointment, Penny thought, as some quivered in mid-air, tipped, and fell back in burning fragments to the earth. And Rio, she thought less happily, would be in ashes by morning.

Faint cries of children floated up from below. "They're calling, '*Cae, cae, balão,*'" Delfina explained. "'Fall down, balloon.' They want to get them for themselves."

"What fun! What else do they do tonight?" Penny turned with relief from thought of the diamond and the message.

"Burn fires and eat. Everyone does that for the next two weeks. Many saints' days come now, and children don't go to school till they are over. But tonight is the best night for balloons."

"Want to forget what we came up to talk about and go round?" Wythe asked. "We might find a balloon or two going up."

"Let's! I'd like to forget forever."

Delfina left with José in the Olivers' car for the Casa. Shortly Wythe and Penny were driving through twisting streets, searching for balloons and fires as eagerly as if they, too, were Brazilian youngsters freed from school for two weeks.

Balloons continued to rise and drift or fall above them, but nowhere could they find one going up. Here and there up dark lanes or in open fields they glimpsed silhouettes of family or neighborhood parties gathered about bonfires.

"The show seems to be over," Wythe said ruefully. "Now if I can find out where we are—"

As he spoke he turned into a street where a great open field was bright with lights and the glow of fires. From the windows of houses overlooking it, people hung out to watch. Hundreds more moved about the field itself.

They parked Wythe's car and strolled over. One glow was a bonfire, burning none too enthusiastically through old boards. A small glow was a fruit crate standing on end, lined with pink tissue paper and lighted with bits of candle to reveal a colored lithograph of the Christ child. That was all Wythe and Penny could see. Perhaps little girls silent in a row before it saw more.

The brightest glow lighted a platform where a young Negro was singing carnival songs to the accompaniment of a tinny banjo. Here the crowd was larger, pressing closely round it to see and hear.

"Let's go," Wythe murmured suddenly in Penny's ear. When they were clear of the crowd he added, "I wish I could be sure it was a pickpocket who went over me. That boy was an expert."

In the car Wythe looked at Penny regretfully. "Hasn't been much of an evening, has it? Would it help if we went up Santa Theresa and looked down from there? It's an interesting old residence section high on a mountain, and its view of the city is something!"

It was an interesting section of steep, cobbled streets, mounting between high stone walls. Stone stairways led upward to large old homes deep in trees. Frequently Wythe stopped for breath-taking glimpses of moonlit city and sea and balloons by the score sailing across the sky.

"Hold tight!" he exclaimed unexpectedly. "We'll make this evening perfect yet. We'll go up Corcovado. Begin polishing up your adjectives."

He drove steadily, winding back and forth on the hair-pin turns, mounting higher and higher. The towering statue of Christ on the summit, luminous in the blast of brilliant floodlights, appeared and disappeared, each glimpse more impressive than the last.

At length they came out on a large cobbled clearing enclosed by a dark railway station and the rim of dark forest.

"This is Paineiras, about halfway up," he explained. "I thought we could get the cable car here. At least I thought it ran till midnight."

"Is it far to the statue? Can't we walk?"

He looked dubiously at her long thin dinner dress and high-heeled green silk slippers. "Could you walk? There is a road for cars, but it's closed at night. Too dangerous."

Penny jumped out to stand beside him. "Of course I can walk."

But a short distance up the road a heavy bar stopped their way. Moved, stubbornly perhaps, to do something determined by themselves instead of by circumstances imposed by others, they stooped under the bar and went on. For the first half-hour they stopped frequently to gaze at the widening world below. After that they moved steadily to keep warm.

Once or twice Penny turned round, thinking she heard a car on the road below, or with the sensation of someone near them. Wythe reassured her.

"There isn't a soul for miles. Few people come up here at night. There are just two fools in this whole country, Penny—you and I."

Up and up they climbed and round and round as the road zigzagged about the mountain. Wythe assured her Corcovado was less than twenty-five hundred feet in height, but on high-heeled evening slippers, using unaccustomed muscles, distance, to Penny, stretched like rubber into miles and miles.

Breathless, her knees trembling, her slippers cutting her heels, she climbed silently, inwardly praying to the *Christo,* always in sight now, to be allowed to lie down and die. Wythe, however, seemed as fresh as when they started, so she pumped herself on and on.

At last they reached steps terraced in stone. The statue, now just above them, was an enormous eye-inspiring figure, standing on a base formed by a white stone structure.

Unexpectedly the steps ended at a dirt clearing where a little wooden shed and a few overturned wheelbarrows offered their view for the one they had struggled to see. But Wythe's blood was up now.

"Wait here. I'll find a way."

Penny waited, shivering in the biting wind. Then shivering again as she heard far below the throb of a climbing car.

"Wythe!" she called.

"Here I am," he answered. "And here's a place to climb up. To the left, Penny."

She ran across the rough ground, but before she could speak he had caught her arm and pulled her up beside him.

"Just a few rough spots here. Then the rest is easy."

"But wait!" she gasped. "A car's coming up, following us. Listen!"

He whirled round to face back down the mountain, listening. There wasn't a sound save the whine of the wind whistling about the statue.

Then they thought no more of cars. Up more steps, past a many-sided pavilion, patronized by bats at that hour, was the statue and the view at last.

White and stern, designed with the greatest economy of line and tremendous power, the *Christo*, formed by thousands of tiny triangles of stone into a great mosaic, reduced them and their affairs to less than the dust whirling about them.

It stood in a circle of powerful lights, dominating city and sea. They looked a long time into the carved face, the outstretched arms, the long, almost fluid folds of the robe falling straight to naked feet.

Then silently they followed the observation platform to the end to gaze on the world before them. Perhaps somewhere else a panorama offered a more magnificent beauty, Penny thought, but on the summit of Corcovado on a night of full moon, she could not imagine it.

At their feet lay the entire city of Rio. Millions of lights like a net of gold flung over valleys and hill slopes were bordered on one side by the endless reaches of the Atlantic and on all the others by the interwoven peaks of the mountains.

Harbor and lakes glimmered beneath the net. Royal palms soared out of it. Picturesque islands in the harbor and off the ivory line of beaches rose dark and mysterious. Ships lying at anchor might have been gold-tipped feathers drifted there from some legendary bird. Above everything arched the night sky and the immensities of space, dwarfing a city of almost two million people to the dimensions of a toy and folding them in a singing silence of wonder and awe.

For Wythe and Penny that silence suddenly was ripped away. From below rose the horrible scream of a man in agony and fear. Fell. Rose again.

Crash after crash followed as something heavy and large hurtled down the mountainside, knocking into boulders, tearing away trees, leaving behind a trail of thundering echoes.

They stopped thinking, stopped breathing. Wordless, motionless, helpless, they listened and strained to look down into that deep valley, black with forests.

Sounds became fewer and fainter. Then did not come at all. In a silence that now seemed to explode in their ears they stood fixed to the ground like the statue above them.

After a time something glowed far down the slope. Grew brighter. Stronger. Soon they could see tongues of flames licking this way and that.

Somehow they returned down the mountain as they had gone up. They passed in silence through alternate stretches of moonlight and shadows. Penny's slippers carved their edges into her feet. Her thin wrap was no protection. But nothing mattered except to reach Wythe's car.

They never reached Wythe's car. They never saw it again.

Though the spot on the cobbled square where he had parked it was filled with moonlight sparkling on broken glass, to them it was empty.

Wythe walked about for a moment while she gazed at the place where the car had stood, as if her looking could bring it back.

"I'm afraid I exaggerated when I told you there were two fools in this country," he said, coming back to her. "They're all rolled into one. And that one is me. Some-one's here."

Out of the darkness a little distance down the road a square, short figure was taking form. And then another, short, too, but with a familiar little swagger. Delfina and José!

Their faces in the moonlight were almost white. As they drew nearer they tried to smile, but only the corners of their lips moved. Delfina found four words: "We've got the car."

Silently Penny and Wythe followed them down the road. In a little clearing off a side road José had concealed the Olivers' car. They sank down on the back seat, still speechless.

José never spoke, though the back of his head was eloquent as he guided the car swiftly round the curves. But Delfina spoke for both of them. Turning on Penny and Wythe with blazing eyes, she spared no words.

"You might have been killed," she concluded at last. "Those men were hunting for you."

"Men! What men?" Wythe demanded.

"The men in the car that followed you—that stole your car."

"I think we'd better wait until we reach my apartment to get this story straight," he interrupted. "And thanks for the scolding, Delfina. It was a peach. I'll remember it all my life."

And I'll remember all my life, Penny thought, this little Brazilian chauffeur and Delfina who, scared to death, stayed by us on that lonely mountain.

José out of the way in Antonietta's room, asleep almost before he reached the door, Wythe and Penny welcomed the dinner they had scorned a few hours before and listened to Delfina.

"We started home," she began, "then we came back. José told me about a car standing at the foot of Dr. Wythe's street with two men in it. He said it came soon after you went up to Dr. Wythe's apartment, Miss Penny. And it stayed there all the time he was waiting for you. I saw it, too, when we went down. I wasn't sure, but I thought one of the men was Mukerji.

"So I told José to go back. But we were too late. Dr. Wythe's car was just coming out of the street. Before we could reach you the car with the two men started after

you. So we went, too. We could have lost you many times.
You turned so often. But that car did not lose you, and we
stayed behind it.

"When you stopped at the place where the bonfire was
they stopped, too. One of the men followed you over to
the bonfire. José was going to go. Then something else
happened."

Delfina stopped, apparently to look over her words.
She was very proud of her English, and this was her moment to display it.

"A motorcycle came. A man in a uniform was on it.
He stopped at Dr. Wythe's. Then he took something out
of his pocket and opened the door and went inside. Many
people wanted to come to see. He made them go away. He
was more than a policeman. Nobody came close. He was
standing near your car when you came back."

"Why didn't you or José tell us then?" Penny asked.

"Because that motorcycle man was there. We thought
you would stop somewhere and we could tell you."

"Quite right," Wythe encouraged when she paused, embarrassed. "And then?"

"When you drove away the men in the car did, too. So
we followed again."

"And I suppose the motorcycle chap brought up the
rear," Wythe commented dryly. "Quite a procession." He
did not look at Penny, nor she at him.

"No. The motorcycle man went back," literal Delfina
assured him. "I watched him go. We followed you and the
other car up to Santa Theresa. When you started up the
road to Paineiras the other car stopped. We went on down
toward Sylvestre as if we was—were—just riding.

"We did not know what to do. We knew you would not
want police. And to come back to the Fabrica for Mr. Mart
or someone would take two, maybe three hours."

"Right again," Wythe applauded.

Delfina warmed with pleasure.

"When we came back to the Paineiras road the car with the men was not there. José heard a car going up the mountain. He said it was the one. So we went, too—after a little. Nobody was at Paineiras. Just your car, Dr. Wythe. José walked up the road a little. The bar was moved. So he said that car had gone up, and we could hear it sometimes.

"Then we did not know what to do as much as before. We did not think you would walk up to the statue and Miss Penny dressed like that. So José put the car in a dark place and we waited. We thought you would hear that car coming and go out of sight and then come down. But you didn't come. Then, after a long time, we heard a terrible scream and a noise. Did you hear it? We—we thought it was you."

Delfina stopped. Her eyes were large and shadowed again with fear. Penny tried to find words but could not. Neither could Wythe.

"Soon a man from that car came down the hill. He was running. He broke the window in Dr. Wythe's car and got in and went away. José and I didn't do anything. We sat still. We thought if you came down we would take you home. And if you didn't come down we would be there in the morning when the stationmen came. We would get them to go with us for you. That's all."

Delfina's flat voice trailed off into silence. She looked tired, more tired than Penny felt, which was as tired as all the tired people in the world.

Wythe and Penny looked at one another. What could they say or do that would mean anything in return for what Delfina and José had done?

"How much does Delfina know?" Wythe asked Penny. "Have you told her anything?"

Penny shook her head.

"Well, she's a leading lady now in whatever this is about. Suppose I tell her something of what we know, and she can cook up her own explanation for José."

Delfina never turned a hair as Wythe talked. Penny, listening, realized that Delfina accepted Wythe's confidence as a very real reward.

When he finished Delfina rose and went into the living room to the table where he had placed the copy of *Fouché*. "It's the book they want?" she asked, turning round.

"Yes," Wythe said.

"They have it then," she told him and smiled for the first time.

Wythe sprang for the table. *Fouché* was gone. He turned to the bookshelves. *Introduction to Argentina* was still there.

17

Sunrise was flooding the eastern skies with color when José stopped the car before the veranda of the Casa. Slippers in her hands, Penny limped to bed. But physical, mental, and emotional aches permitted only light, fitful slumber throughout the morning and early afternoon.

At sound of her door opening cautiously she stirred and opened her eyes. But no bouncing powder puff pushed in to leap upon her bed. And the eyes that met hers certainly were not Delfina's.

They were pale eyes. And deadly intent. Madge Cochrane's! Before she could sit up the door closed, and she heard light footsteps receding hurriedly down the corridor to the kitchen.

Penelope forced her aching body erect and groped for robe and slippers. But the door opened again, to admit the Baroneza this time and a Delfina angry and concerned.

"Oh!" Penny groaned. "What a time to have callers. Have we a wheel chair, Delfina? I don't think I can walk—"

"She didn't come to call, Miss Penny. And she's gone now," Delfina assured her. "I wish the senhora was home. Mrs. Cochrane wouldn't dare think such things."

Penny sat down, aghast, "Delfina! Mrs. Cochrane wasn't looking for her husband again? Here!"

The maid nodded, then said more cheerfully, "But I don't think she'll come back. She felt awful when you saw her. And she looked awful, too, Miss Penny. She's going to be sick if she doesn't stop worrying."

Baroneza, however had no concern for Penny's aches and misgivings. A glorious day was made for walks, she implied, following Penny about, nudging her, barking, sitting up to beg with eyes and paws. At last pity moved Penny. She had neglected the little tyrant, she admitted guiltily.

In the soft light of the waning afternoon they set out. But before the Casa gates were reached Penny slipped off the Baroneza's leash. After Corcovado her feet simply could not stand the pace.

Like an arrow, the Baroneza sped down the hill to the high ground above the laboratories. Too late Penny saw that Mart had had the long grass burned over there on Saturday. By the time she arrived the dog's snowy coat was already black with grime, her plume a gray and clotted brush.

Wearily she watched while the excited Baroness dashed back and forth after butterflies or, diverted by one or another of the strange objects the fire had revealed, investigated with a busy nose. Her own curiosity aroused, Penny moved gingerly over the burned field to investigate, too.

One rounded little object proved to be a brick oven, its iron door hanging loose on a single pin. Another appeared to be an old grave, placed between the trunks of three coco palms. About four feet square, with three stone walls a foot high and a fourth twice that, it had obviously been neglected for years. Inside the little walls lay a motley collection of old iron scrap, broken glass, and bits of wood, drifted over with singed leaves and grass. More interesting were the low guava, acacia, and cashew trees now standing free of high grass. Strangely shaped seed pods and, occasionally, small pouch-shaped birds' nests dangled from frail twigs.

After a time she missed the Baroneza, but in the quiet of the deserted grounds, placid now in the thinning light of the sun, she could hear her. Penny looked about uneasily. The Baroneza was not barking; rather, emitting a curious assortment of whines and growls.

Following the sounds, she arrived at the rim of the plateau above the laboratories. Below her Baroneza was running back and forth before their own varnished doors. Sniffing. Jumping against them. Whining, growling.

Still dull from her experience on Corcovado, Penny watched idly for a time. Through a high window she could see the sunlight falling across the tops of file cases lining the wall between office and laboratories.

Something about their position startled her alert. They were not straight as she had seen them on Friday, but pulled out from the wall in a disorderly slant.

Then she was down beside the Baroneza, alternately pounding on the doors and listening. No sound or movement answered her. Yet someone must be inside or the Baroneza would have passed right by. And the only one who could be there on Sunday was Wythe.

From that level the windows were high above her head. Running round to the back of the building, she found a large empty crate. By pulling and pushing she managed to propel it to a side window of the office and climbed up.

Wythe was not inside. Neither was this his orderly office. Every drawer of every file was pulled out, and papers by deep on the floor. Desk drawers were turned upside down on top of them.

Twisted across the corner of the north wall was the bookcase. Its books, too, were sprawled in tumbled heaps on the floor, as if someone had looked at each one, then hurled it down.

As she gazed, stupefied, at the havoc some papers that had slipped down before the inner doors to the laboratories stung her eyes. A dark stain spread among them.

"Wythe! Wythe!" she screamed and pounded idiotically on the window. Only the derisive hoot of an engine pulling a freight train into the hills answered her.

Jumping down, she tugged the crate to the next window to look into the main laboratory. There the chaos was indescribable. Tables and cabinets were bare, their contents a littered mass of broken glass, powders, and apparatus on the floor.

But her eyes did not linger there. They went to the body of a man lying face down just inside the doors to Wythe's office. Penelope's face darkened with incredulity, then horrified recognition. Mr. Cochrane! There was no mistaking that bald head, the plump, smooth hands, a diamond gleaming dully on one.

Sobbing in reaction and horror, she jumped down and fled for the Casa, the Baroneza close to her heels. The realization as she ran that the watchman would begin his rounds at six gave wings to her feet. It was already nearly five.

"Get Wythe out here," she cried as Delfina appeared in the kitchen door. "Tell him to go straight to the laboratories."

When the first watchman came round a little after six Wythe and Penny were standing in the laboratories pathway, watching the sunset. They returned his polite *"Boa tarde"* as politely. Assured by Wythe's presence that all was well with the building, he passed on up the pavement to the factories.

They watched until he was safely on his way, then turned slowly to the varnished doors. Without a word Wythe unlocked them and stepped inside. Penny followed.

The light was dim now, and the chaos on the floor a mass of gray-and-black shadows. When Wythe flashed on the lights he stood beside the switch, his eyes darkening.

He had worked more than a year to build these laboratories and start them functioning, Penny thought, watching him. But if he was thinking that he said nothing of it. When he spoke his voice was as quiet as ever.

"I'm going to open those doors."

"I'm staying."

Stepping across papers and desk drawers, he opened the doors a little, swung them wide. Penny followed his glance to the floor.

No crumpled body lay there. No dark stain spread over the floor. Only a single paper near the doors showed one corner dimly red. Beyond them the confusion of twisted equipment and broken glass glimmered here and there in the light from the office.

Penny gasped, but Wythe made no sound. He stood rigidly erect, his eyes fixed on the floor. Then slowly, stiffly, like a man walking in his sleep, he moved down the room. He did not speak, did not touch anything but the curtains at the windows which he closed one by one.

After a moment Penny turned away and sat down in his chair behind his desk in the office. She could not bear to watch him.

Her own mind was numb. Yet beneath it somehow a mass of thoughts was whirling—phrases, names, bits of ideas, memories. They moved fantastically in and out, combining ridiculously, formed at last into a meaningless sequence—"A two-o'clock man, a two-o'clock man." Two o'clock! She repeated the phrase idly, then shook herself back to reality.

Two days before at two o'clock she had sat at this desk looking at two pieces of glass lying side by side, the little Unprotecting Arm between them.

"Wythe!" she cried.

He appeared in the doorway, the laboratories dark now behind him. In the strong office light, his face was gray and ridged with deeper gray lines across his forehead.

She hesitated, then as he continued to question her silently she asked. "The samples of glass, the Unprotecting Arm—where are they?"

"Safe in a lockbox in my bank downtown. I took them in Friday after I showed them to you. Why?"

"I thought whoever did this might have learned about them somehow—might know what we know about that man on the Casa steps."

He shook his head. "We're the only ones who could know that. No, I think it is the message they are hunting."

Moving round the wreckage to the desk, he twisted *Introduction to Argentina* from his pocket and laid it before her.

"What's that for? I mean, why did you bring it here?"

"I'm expecting visitors again in my apartment." His lips twisted wryly. "I thought it might be safe here till morning. It seems I am mistaken."

Snapping the office window curtains together on their rods, he picked up the book. "Let's go. Nothing more we can do here."

"Leave all this? Can't we—?"

"No, we can't." His voice was brittle.

"Well, I can." Penny jumped up. "I'm going to put those books back and pick up the papers, at least."

She plunged in, hoping desperately he would help her. Her laboratory hadn't been destroyed, but she knew something of what he felt. For hours, it seemed, she picked up books at random, smoothed their pages, and placed them on shelves in the double silence of Sunday evening and his remoteness.

"You're mixing them up," he said, suddenly beside her. "You straighten them out and give them to me. I'll put them in place."

Neither of them thought of dinner or Delfina. Neither of them mentioned the stain on the floor. Wythe worked silently while Penny chattered on and on about anything that came into her head. As they were picking up the last papers she remembered her discoveries in the burned grass.

"You must see this grave," she babbled brightly. "It must be very old. It's like nothing I've ever seen before. Come *now*. It's only a step from the laboratories."

Except for the lights on the hills and along the Fabrica pavement the night was as black as velvet when they opened the doors.

"Going to rain," Wythe said. "Wait. I'll get a flash—if there is one."

He turned back while she applauded her own skill as a psychologist. His voice was back to normal. He moved less like a man in a nightmare.

"Do you know what time it is?" he asked when he returned. "After ten. Hungry? Look here, isn't this the night I invited you to dinner?"

"You gave it to me last night, remember? Then showed me Corcovado. I'll reverse it tonight. Show you the grave, then feed you."

"This works, anyway," he said, snapping on the flash.

"Oh, you'll probably find a lot of salvage in the morning," she assured him as they climbed the steps cut in the bank to the plateau.

At the top he stopped her, a hand on her arm, the flash dark. "Hear anything?"

She listened. "Not a sound. Why?"

He did not answer for a moment. When he did his voice was low, hesitant. "This is as safe a place as any to tell you—" She felt his hand grow hard on her arm. "If I should tell you."

That familiar tremor of cold ran over Penny. "Wythe," she whispered, "do you know who—?"

"No. I don't know. Remember that, Penny. But perhaps you should know I came out to the laboratories early this afternoon—to work. Cock dropped in. He—he was furiously angry about something—and he was looking for— for Mart."

Mart! Thought of that irascible redhead, of his contempt for Mr. Cochrane's methods rocked Penny. A meeting between those two—both angry— Another thought rocked her as drastically.

"Wythe," she whispered again. "Madge—his wife—was out here, too, looking for him."

"For Mart?"

"No, for her husband. She thought he was at the Casa— with me. Her eyes—they were terrible."

Wythe's hand closed like a vise on her arm. "Let's see that grave and get out of this," he said clearly. Then, as they moved through the matted stubble, he added in a lower tone, "This thing's gone beyond us, Penny. The less we say and know, the better. O.K.?"

"O.K." She turned in relief. "Here's the grave."

He swung the light on it, then up to her face. "This life is getting you." He smiled almost naturally at her. "That's no grave. It's a *tanque*—an old-fashioned Brazilian water trough. There were plenty of them around this section once. Paul saved as many of the old trees and things as he could in laying out these grounds. He likes them."

While he talked Wythe continued to hold the light on the old iron and glass in the trough. Suddenly he darkened it.

"That stuff looks as if it had been there for years, doesn't it? And probably will be for years more. No one on the property would ever think of cleaning out a place like this of his own accord."

"Probably not," Penny answered carelessly. "Shall we go now?"

"Wait a moment." He stooped down and touched the debris. "How about burying *Argentina* until tomorrow under this junk? No one would think of looking for it here in a thousand years."

"I wish it were a well. Then it wouldn't matter if they did. Go ahead."

Penny held the flash while he bent down to lift out some of the scrap.

"Turn it on. Hold it low." He exclaimed, "Look!"

She flashed on the light and looked. His hands, deep among crevices, were holding something solid. He took the flash and held it close to the mass.

"Look! This isn't old junk accumulated over years and lying here for more. It's one of the cleverest things I've ever seen. All these pieces are soldered together—they're solid."

"The Brazilian climate," Penny told him. "Everything grows here."

"Not this stuff," he declared, still peering into it. "It's an expert job, beautifully done. But why? Hold the flash again—

Stooping over the *tanque,* he slipped his fingers among the crevices, began to straighten slowly, lifting as he rose until he could lift no farther.

The solid mass of debris came up with him for a distance, then tipped back against the higher wall of the trough. Its foundation was a heavy wooden base like a trapdoor.

Darkness, blacker than the night's, lay where it had been. Cautiously Wythe explored it with the flash. A steep stairway of narrow stone steps led downward.

"Not in a thousand years, eh?" Wythe laughed shortly. "I think, lady, I was about to place *Argentina* on the door-step of the secret entrance to the Fabrica we have been looking for!"

He added quickly. "I'll take you back to the Casa."

"And where are you going?"

"What do you think?"

"Not down those steps without me. If you go, so do I."

"Nonsense!" Wythe hesitated, said abruptly, "Come on, then. Why not? There's probably no danger at this time on Sunday night. And I may not get another chance as good."

He was descending as he spoke, his flashlight exploring the steps. Penny, her heart racing, was right behind him.

Perhaps a dozen steps down they came to solid ground and stood in a narrow passage, roughly paved and walled with stone. As far as the flash could penetrate the black-ness, those walls ran on and on, glistening with moisture where light touched them. The air was dank with it and warm.

"Whew!" Wythe took of his coat and folded it over his arm. "Still with me?"

"Yes," Penny gasped and mentally thanked Corcovado for the flat-soled canvas sneakers she was wearing.

They moved on slowly, following the blur of light the flash threw before them. Suddenly it went dark.

"What's the matter?" Penny's teeth were chattering in spite of her effort to control them.

"Nothing," Wythe murmured. "I don't know how long this flash is good for. We may need it more later. Take my hand and keep touching the wall with your left. I will, too, on this side."

Guided by hands and feet, they crept ahead. *Introduction to Argentina,* in the pocket of Wythe's coat, nudging her occasionally, was the only variation in the monotony of dampish stone under her feet, dampish stone under her hand.

After a time she moved automatically, her mind returning to the wrecked laboratories and the problems they raised. They had told no one but Delfina anything of what had happened. It would be impossible to tell anyone what she had seen this afternoon, what they suspected. But something would have to be said to explain that destruction.

Her feet stopped, though her thoughts went on.

"What is it?"

"I—I don't know," she began. Then knew quickly. "My hand isn't touching wall. Just empty space."

He stood rigid a moment, pressing her hand in warning. "Hear anything?"

They might have been sealed in their graves; perhaps they were, Penny thought wildly. Out on the prairies and high in the Rockies she had known silence, but nothing like this entombment that enclosed them now.

Cautiously Wythe stooped, pulling her down with him, and snapped on the flash for an instant. There was no wall beside her because it had been cut away to form a rough arch that opened into a small stone-walled enclosure. Beyond the arch the wall continued again.

They peered into the room, the flashlight picking out rusted rings set among the stones of wall and floor.

"Nice little place—" Wythe's murmur stopped.

Words on Penelope's lips froze, too. For the moving light, circling the floor to the corner beside her, was resting on the body of Mr. Cochrane! It appeared to have been placed carefully on a bed of old clothes.

As the light of the flash moved over it she stood fixed. The light had picked up something else almost at her feet. A heavy gold blob on a length of slender black cane projected beyond the pile of clothing!

She had seen that cane swinging jauntily in the hand of the second Dr. Rosario on the decks of the *Paraguay*. She had seen it raised to strike!

"Wythe!" she tried to whisper, could not. Turning, she touched his arm. It was hard as stone. He appeared stone-like, too, and utterly unaware of her or where they were. He was looking at the still face of the U.E. president.

"Wythe," she tried again. "That cane! I know whose it is. Those gray tweeds, too."

Still he did not answer, and she had to find an explanation for herself. It came—to turn her almost as rigid and still as Wythe.

She heard again his words by Pot Seven, explaining how a man's body had been destroyed there, heard him say, half to himself, "I wonder what became of the clothes."

The clothes were here. Then the man on the steps of the Casa, the man whose body had been destroyed, must have been the false Dr. Rosario!

As the knowledge formed in her mind Wythe swung round toward the archway. If Penny had not seized his hand so tightly he could not move without her; he would have left her there, she knew. Obviously he knew nothing, thought of nothing but reaching the man or men responsible for Emmett Cochrane's death.

In the passage, the flash dark again, she dug her toes into a crevice between the stones and brought him to a stop.

"Let's go back—get help, Wythe—the police—someone—"

"I'm going on."

"But we can't! We'll be killed—like—" His hand, crushing hers, silenced her.

She heard then faint sounds in the passage. They came from the direction of the *tanque* entrance. Behind them. Rapid, padding little sounds.

The next moment Wythe had drawn her back through the archway, thrust her into a corner. He released her then, but she could feel him standing in front of her, tight as a coiled spring.

The sounds died. Silence beat on their ears in roaring waves. The dank, warm air stifling.

At some change in Wythe she peered round at the archway. A pencil of light was creeping across the sunken stone threshold. It flicked, went out! Someone stood outside! Watching for them? Waiting?

A minute dragged by. Another. And another. Penny hardly breathed. Wythe made no sign of life whatever. Suddenly she began to shiver. The damp stone at her back, she thought, was chilling her through and through. Wythe's hand groped back, found hers, and pressed it warningly.

Still they waited. No sound from the passage. No sound anywhere. She lost all sense of time. Lost even her power to feel, to think. Knew only a sensation that this was how it fell to be buried alive.

She came back to reality to find Wythe holding her, saying over and over in her ear, "Let's go, Penny. O.K.?"

She pressed his hand and they crept forward to the archway. To her amazement Wythe did not turn back toward the *tanque*. But she made no protest. None seemed worth making.

And so as if they had never paused at the little room with the rusted rings they went on up the passage. Shortly she knew they were climbing and steeply. Muscles that still ached from Corovado's road began to protest again.

Then their feet-struck solid stone. A cautious reconnaissance with their hands revealed steps before them, leading almost straight up.

"Make it without the flash?" Wythe whispered.

Feeling their way, they moved up awkwardly. At last their hands plunged into space, and exploring, found a broad stone there. Standing on it, they listened while Wythe investigated the wall, found a door.

Their ears found something else. Voices on the other side of the door—two, possibly more. They appeared to be arguing or fighting. Once Penny thought she heard a woman's voice rise hysterically. Then one voice rose above the others.

Wythe, pressed closely against the door, made a sharp motion with the hand to which Penny clung. "Quiet!" he breathed, although she was already like a deaf-mute. To her astonishment he released her hand and began to beat the door with the flashlight, heedless of splintering glass.

"Dr. Attilio!" he shouted. "Sousa!"

Dr. Attilio! That hidden entrance and secret tunnel led to his door! Between relief and apprehension, while Wythe continued to shout and pound, she tried to penetrate the blackness behind them. But no pencil of light showed there. Could she have imagined it?

Silence was now as thick on the other side of the door as it had been in the tunnel. Shortly came the muffled sound of something heavy being moved, the clang of heavy metal. Finally a familiar and resonant voice called, *"Um momento!"*

18

A creaking, then a sliver of light, then a glare. The heavy door swung inward, lifting as it went a tapestry that extended like a tent roof over their heads as they entered.

Dr. Attilio stood to one side, staring at them in amazement.

"Dr. Sloane! Wythe! Come in! Come in! And Miss Paget!"

He let the heavy door swing back, swung some sort of bolt into place, and dropped the tapestry. Wiping perspiration from his forehead, he turned to wave them to chairs, to sink into one himself.

"How did you find that old *subterraneo?*" he asked after a moment.

Dizzy from the warm air in the tunnel, dazzled by the lights, Penelope did not listen. Gradually the room became clear, a rich room lighted by several reading lamps of delicately hued fishskin and molded metals.

On three sides bookshelves alternating with old tapestries and wide, high windows mounted to a lofty ceiling of dark, shining wood, elaborately carved. Across from her in the fourth wall two polished doors led into other parts of the house. But her glance merely paused on them.

For between them a magnificent pair of gilded metal gates almost sealed a tall archway. Above them she could

see the vaulted ceiling of a chapel and, between the openings in their design, the points of four candles twinkling
far back in dimness.

As her eyes followed the baroque pattern of the gates
upward she repressed the exclamation of recognition that
rose to her lips. Above the arch a fragment of ancient and
faded tapestry protected by glass was not in itself start-
ling, but a single detail of its design riveted her attention. Worked in gold was the lower portion of a right arm;
worked in silver, a tightly folded fist!

Her eyes remained on it as she listened to Wythe explaining glibly, "I didn't find the *subterraneo*. Miss Paget
came across it this afternoon while wandering over that
high ground above the laboratories. She though it was a
grave, and to prove to her it was a *tanque,* I tried to lift
out some junk accumulated there. Everything stuck together, naturally came up in one piece as I pulled. Below
were steps, and here we are."

"So you are." Patting his forehead with his wadded
handkerchief, Dr. Attilio smiled again. "And very welcome, too. May I offer you something to eat, to drink—a
highball, wine perhaps?"

"Thank you, no." Wythe refused quickly for both of
them. "We just left the Casa a moment to see the grave. If
I don't get Miss Paget home soon Delfina will call out the
Brazilian equivalent of the marines."

Penny listened with increasing incredulity and relief.
This pleasantly chatting Wythe, smoking a cigarette as he
talked, appeared completely at ease. He was not the same
man at all who had entered the tunnel, stopped at that
little room, come on, in spite of all she could do, to the
door now hidden by tapestry.

Dr. Attilio, too, outwardly at least, was controlling
admirably his surprise at their unusual manner of arrival.
He leaned back against the deep carving of his chair,

placed at one side of the gilded gates. His fine bearing, well-placed voice—everything about him, she thought—reflected generations of wealth and position and security.

But as she looked at him she saw perspiration start again on his forehead. He appeared alert, as if listening or conscious of someone or something near by. Puzzled, she turned to Wythe. He seemed unaware or unconcerned. His eyes were fixed in open interest on the gilded gates.

"You are fortunate to have found me in this room at this hour," Dr. Attilio was saying. "I doubt if anyone else in the house remembers that old *subterraneo*. I had almost forgotten it myself and had to lift each tapestry before I found the right one."

He turned to Penny. "You will be interested to know it was built before my grandfather's time. In those days Rio was far away. This was lonely country. It was necessary to have a way to leave the house quickly or, if men were in the fields, to get them back."

"Are there just two entrances?" Wythe asked. "The one here, the other through that *tanque?*"

"That's all there are now. There were two more somewhere around the foot of this hill, but they were long ago effaced. Workmen's homes and shops stand on them now. I wouldn't even know where to look for them.

"You like that fragment of old tapestry above my chapel?" he asked, turning back to Penny. "It was brought to Brazil by my ancestor, Francisco de Sousa, a fidalgo of the Royal House of Portugal, in the seventeenth century. Sousas ever since have played important roles in Brazil, as a colony of Portugal, as a monarchy, and in the establishment of the Republic. But now we've turned to less spectacular fields—industry, science, even the arts."

Pride crept into his voice and manner. "That is our coat of arms. Of course, with the Republic, we think no more of titles in Brazil, I still treasure that bit of banner

Francisco de Sousa brought with him more than two and a half centuries ago."

Dr. Attilio appeared now to be talking against time, as if he wished to keep them there. Embarrassed, too, by his reference to personal things, he turned to Wythe. "You must tell me about the *subterraneo*. I have not been in it since I was a child."

"We can't tell you much," Wythe assured him. "My flashlight wasn't too good and died after a short distance. I felt our way along with my hand on the wall to the right. It led us straight to your door."

Incredulity flashed in Dr. Attilio's face, was gone. "You came through that *subterraneo* in the dark! And you, Miss Penny, you were not afraid?"

"Paralyzed," she confessed. "But excited, too. I'd never been in a secret passage before."

She longed to ask questions. But Wythe's explanation had omitted so much she was afraid to risk a word. Glancing about for a cigarette, she found a silver box inviting her on the table at her elbow. She smiled as she opened it and paused before taking a cigarette to look at the large rough piece of milky glass that stood beside it.

If Dr. Attilio had not been a glassman it would have been incongruous in a room so rich. But she knew what it represented. In India Paul had treasured another unlovely piece of glass—the first made in the glass factory he set up there.

"You discovered me in a—a private session with myself," Dr. Attilio was telling Wythe when she turned to listen again. "That is why you heard my voice in this room. You Americans flatter me so about my English that I take pains to keep it up to the mark."

He indicated a radio on a nearby bookshelf. "Every night about this time London broadcasts a forum on some phase of the war. I listen and answer with my own opinions. Perhaps you heard me voicing somewhat strong views—"

"No," Wythe told him quickly. "We could hear no words. I thought I recognized your voice and took a chance. And now I think I must take Penny back to the Casa."

Penny rose at once, sure he should. Nothing in the words or manner of either man could disturb anyone, but Wythe, she knew, was lying. She felt sure Dr. Attilio was, too. He had not been alone in that room. They had heard more than one voice speaking. Besides, her chair had been warm when she sank into it, and Dr. Attilio obviously preferred that large, high-backed, formal chair to a low, soft one.

"You must let me send you home, then." Dr. Attilio rose. As he moved toward a bell rope he added, "But first Dr. Sloane must put on his coat."

Wythe laughed and turned to the chest behind Penny where he had dropped it. "I'd forgotten all about it."

Dr. Attilio followed him to pick up the flashlight lying on top of it. Penny forced herself to remain quiet while Wythe leisurely shook himself into his coat. She understood now why he had splintered the light.

"You expected to read Miss Penny an appropriate sonnet at the grave?"

They both looked up to see Dr. Attilio's eyes fixed on the book in Wythe's pocket. Wythe laughed and patted *Introduction to Argentina.*

"I'd forgotten this, too. I brought it to the Casa to—to settle an argument with Penny."

"And what book can do that?" Dr. Attilio extended his hand.

Wythe hesitated, drew it out. "You won't approve," he warned.

"Introduction to Argentina!" Dr. Attilio decidedly did not approve. "You live in Brazil and read about the Argentine, Dr. Sloane?"

Penny looked steadily at the Brazilian. "Doesn't the Good-Neighbor Policy work in South America, too?"

Dr. Attilio did not change expression, but his hand tightened on the book. "Of course, Miss Penny. With your permission, Wythe, I will read this book."

Wythe, studying Penny with hardly concealed surprise, and Dr. Attilio both turned at her stifled exclamations. She was facing the gilded gates, her eyes wide.

When first she had looked through those gates the points of four burning candles had been visible. Now two had vanished, then reappeared as the two on the opposite side blacked out. Against their tiny aura of light a dark silhouette was moving. Coming toward the gates.

"Penny!" Wythe shook her arm. "For heaven's sake, don't faint now. You're all right. If Dr. Attilio will ring for his car I'll have you home in ten minutes." The pressure on her arm tightened painfully.

Then his hand dropped and he swung around. They all did, startled into immobility. A thunderous knocking, though muffled, rolled through the room. It came from behind the tapestry that concealed the door to the tunnel.

Dr. Attilio was the first to move. He turned to Wythe. "I did wrong to keep you here so long. Now I'm afraid it is too late." He lifted the tapestry, motioning to Wythe to hold it up for him. As he disappeared behind it Penny returned, shaken, to his chair.

Again she heard the clatter of the heavy bolt. Again the creaking protest as the massive door swung inward. Wythe, she could see, was alert and uneasy. The sight did not calm her own tingling nerves.

A moment more and Mart stepped into the room. The door closed, and Dr. Attilio appeared behind him. Wythe dropped the tapestry and stepped back to Penny's chair, stooping over it to take a cigarette from the box beside her.

"Careful," he murmured. "Mart—in tunnel—behind us." He straightened to light his cigarette and stroll back to his chair.

Mart's glance went over them, but he said nothing. He continued to look about the room, then turned questioningly to Dr. Attilio.

"Sit down, Mart. You, too, Wythe." Dr. Attilio returned to his own chair, dabbing again at his forehead.

"Thanks, I'll stand if you don't mind. I think better on my feet." Mart stepped back against the tapestry, folded his arms across his chest, his right hand inside his coat.

"A telephone's on that chest behind Penny, Wythe. Hold the receiver when you get the connection so that I can talk. I've just discovered how Mario got those lamps out."

Wythe did not move. "So have we," he said coolly, "but that tunnel will still be there tomorrow."

"Mart, is this necessary?" Dr. Attilio protested. Before Mart's belligerency he shrugged. "Please do as he asks, Wythe."

While Wythe slowly dialed Penny sat motionless, her eyes fixed unseeingly on the gilded gates. In her amazement at Mart's arrival, the electricity he had brought into the room with him, she had forgotten the figure she had glimpsed behind them.

She was too accustomed now to Mart's inevitable appearance at crucial moments to be surprised to find him emerging from the tunnel. Or to realize it had been his flash that had thrown that pencil of light. But his manner now was amazing. He seemed to feel he held a leading role in this tangle in which they were all caught.

Certainly he was something more than an aggressive young man now. He was dangerous, and both Dr. Attilio and Wythe knew it!

Her eyes focused suddenly on the gates. Someone moved there. A white blur of hand was rising. In one of the openings a small dark ring appeared against the gold. As she watched, mesmerized, it disappeared to appear an instant later a little higher at a larger space. It was pointed straight at Mart, standing above Wythe at the telephone behind her.

Afraid to cry a warning, she held her breath. Then her hand went out casually to the little table. Lingered over the cigarette box, flashed to close about the lump of glass.

The crash as it struck merged with the thunder of a shot. For a space that seemed timeless nothing moved in the room save a curling plume of smoke rising toward the ceiling and the soft plopping of glass fragments falling on the deep rug.

Mart leaped in front of her, his own revolver naked in his hand.

Dr. Attilio sprang up, too. He moved swiftly to the gates, turned a key in the large, anciently shaped lock. No sound came front behind them. The four candle points flickered steadily.

Wythe's level, cool voice sounded loud in the silence. "Here's your connection, Mart."

"Hang up," Mart ordered curtly. "I don't want it now."

Silently Wythe replaced the receiver, returned to his chair. Mart took another near him. Silence closed over the room.

Penny's fright turned to wonder. No one seemed concerned or even to remember that shot from the gates!

Her eyes traveling slowly from one face to another saw each intent on the same spot on the rug. But when she turned her own gaze there all she could see was scattered bits of glass.

Gradually one stood out from the rest. While the others sparkled with a thin translucence in the light of the tall lamps on either side of the gates, this appeared dull, hard, and heavy. Here and there a gray patina or frosting covered it, rendering it unresponsive to the light.

Or was it? As her eyes remained on it they caught deep within it a miniature fire. Tiny blue rays shot out from it in a radiance of pure light of its own.

Understanding ran over her in cold waves and up into her throat and face. The diamond! That dull blob as long and wide as an egg and at least half as thick must be Satan's Sixth Finger!

Unconsciously she leaned forward. Mart's voice thrust her back. "Sit still. Don't touch it."

He rose, eyes watchful, hand firm on his revolver. Walking over, he scooped it up and into a pocket, returned as watchfully to his chair.

"Yes, Miss Penny," Dr. Attilio said heavily. "Satan's Sixth Finger. After a century of peace it returns to carry on its tradition of death." He appeared shaken by some emotion he fought to conceal. "Heaven forgive me, if sheltering it in this house—"

Sheltering! Penny's thought returned to that invisible figure sheltered in the chapel. She shivered. Wythe rose immediately.

"You should be home, Penny."

"Sit down, Sloane." Mart's voice was crisp, final. "If Penny can climb Corcovado she can sit in a chair for a few minutes."

"But why? What in—?"

"Sit down!"

19

Hours seemed to pass as they sat in that pregnant silence, their eyes seldom straying now from those gilded gates. At last a car, several by the sound, stopped outside. Dr. Attilio rose, hesitated, then after a glance at Mart opened one of the smaller doors.

A blur of footsteps sounded in the corridor. A quick voice gave some order. Then a dark and slender man with hair so black and smooth it appeared lacquered on his head entered the room. Penny stiffened in recognition. The detective, the man who had rescued her—years ago, it seemed now—from Senhor Rodrigo!

He stopped just inside the door to look about. He recognized Dr. Attilio with a nod, Penny with another. Then he turned to Mart and Wythe.

Mart said, "We've met before, Lieutenant. Dr. Wythe Sloane, Lieutenant Diego Machado, of the Policia Central. Dr. Sloane is director of laboratories—"

"Of course. I know Dr. Sloane by reputation very well. Sit down, all of you." The lieutenant started to walk briskly into the room.

"Watch your step," Mart warned. "Broken glass."

Lieutenant Diego looked down, thrust some fragments aside with a foot, and turned to face them. "Who fired that shot? A telephone operator reported hearing one."

No one answered.

As he waited his eyes moved from face to face. Mart, Dr. Attilio, and Wythe looked at him steadily. Penny, blankly.

"Perhaps it was the crash of glass that was heard, Lieutenant," Dr. Attilio suggested quietly. "It could have sounded like a shot."

"Perhaps," Lieutenant Diego agreed dryly. "Since no one appears to have been hurt, we can discuss that later. While I'm here, Dr. Attilio, I'd like to see and discuss—"

A slow smile moved over Dr. Attilio's lips. "The matter has passed out of my hands, Lieutenant." His eyes indicated Mart.

"So? Then perhaps we three can discuss it. First, one question for Dr. Sloane, and then I think we can excuse him and Miss Paget. What is your interest in Satan's Sixth Finger, Dr. Sloane?"

Wythe smiled. "Perhaps I shouldn't say I have no interest in it. Certainly I'm curious to see so fabulous a stone. Outside of that, it means nothing to me—personally."

"Yet you have been more or less active in various events connected with it, haven't you?"

"I'd have to know specifically what you mean by 'events,'" Wythe's quiet voice countered. "Certainly several unexpected 'events' have occurred around here during the past week. I've been more or less an innocent bystander—even Boy Scout—trying to do what I could—"

"For one, Dr. Sloane, we have reason to think a man disappeared within the walls of Fabrica da Luz last Wednesday night. He was traced to the north gate. But has not been seen since. Can you tell us anything of him?"

"I know a man was murdered inside the Fabrica walls Wednesday night," Wythe assured him. "I can tell you everything about his murder—except his name."

At the immediate response in the detective's face Wythe amended hastily, "Not here—at this moment. Though with

Miss Paget's aid I could tell you what happened. Or, if you will give me a little time to prepare some formulas, I can tell you—with proofs."

"Splendid. And you, Miss Paget, you will confirm Dr. Sloane's statement?"

Penny hesitated, plunged. "Yes, Lieutenant Diego. And I know the name of the murdered man." As Wythe's amazed glance turned on her she added, "I—I just learned tonight—"

"Penny, you little fool!" Mart shouted. "If you hadn't saved my life tonight I'd—" His pause was angry too. "There was a shot fired, Lieutenant. It was meant for me. Miss Paget may not know who fired it, but if she hadn't thrown a chunk of glass at those gates you might have found me on the rug."

The detective spun round, but Dr. Attilio reached the gates before him, stood with his back to them.

"I have given sanctuary in my chapel to Mrs. Cochrane, Lieutenant Diego," he said firmly. "And with your permission I should like to give her the sanctuary of my home tonight. She is terrified, almost out of her mind with remorse. And she can harm no one else."

"Mrs. Cochrane!" Wythe sprang up, amazed and concerned.

"Dr. Attilio"—the detective spoke quickly—"you will see that Miss Paget is taken home at once, please. There are cars outside. Then return here."

"I'll take Miss Paget home," Wythe interrupted.

"One moment, Dr. Sloane. In Miss Paget and yourself I have found two valuable sources of information. As soon as we have arranged a time when I may see your proofs and formulas I am sending you to your home under escort also. Good night, Miss Paget. Unfortunately we must meet again."

Dr. Attilio's hand was already on Penny's arm, propelling her forward. She went without protest, grateful to get away. All she wanted now was to reach the Casa, to be alone to sort out the events that had piled up so madly upon her. Perhaps then she could discover the source of the terrible fear that gripped her.

The night air, fresh and cooled with rain, was soothing after the smoke-and-powder-scented room. She sank back against the seat of the police car in which Dr. Attilio placed her and filled her lungs. He talked in Portuguese with the police-chauffeur but said not a word to her. And she could make nothing of his inscrutable face as she was driven away.

When the brief, swift drive was over and the car roaring up the hill to the Casa gates she saw with dismay that her longing for quiet was not to be gratified. The house was brightly lighted. From every window sounded the Baroneza's frenzied barks.

The car stopped before the veranda steps. Dreading to enter the Casa alone now, she descended slowly, expecting the police-chauffeur to drive away. Instead, he came round to stand beside her while he clapped his hands loudly.

The doors of the living room flew open. Paul and Eleanor appeared in them, silhouetted against the lights inside.

At least Penny thought she saw them. But when next she opened her eyes she was in her own bed in her own room, and the sun was pouring through her windows. As she sat up a now familiar nose thrust her door open, and a spotless powder puff leaped up beside her.

Paul and Eleanor—the old, real Paul and Eleanor of India—followed to regard her with anxious smiles.

"I did see you!" Penny cried. "I wanted you so much I was afraid I'd dreamed you."

"Darling!" Eleanor sat down beside her and held her close. "You frightened us almost to death."

"Coming home at all hours, with a policeman in tow, to pass out in our arms!" Paul accused her. "And dirtier than the Baroneza ever was."

"Miss Penny is worse than the Baroneza, Mr. Paul." Delfina with a breakfast tray joined the spectators around the bed. "Every time she goes out she gets into trouble." She placed the tray beside Penny, picked up the Baroneza, and departed.

"Well!" Eleanor looked after her. "At least you've completely won our Delfina. Eat your breakfast now while we tell you our good news. Jay is safe in New York, safe and returning to Rio by plane within a week."

"Your Pepperpot located him in Bellevue Hospital," Paul added. "He'd been doped, Penny, half poisoned, the night you saw him. The police found him the day after you sailed, unconscious, in an abandoned cellar near the water front. An awful looking place. Pepperpot—what a name!—notified the U.E. and they had him transferred to a private hospital."

"You saw him?"

"The poor thing is still addled," Paul exclaimed, shaking his head. "No my dear, we've not been to New York. Lieutenant Diego Machado saw to that."

"We've been held incommunicado in Rio since Wednesday morning," Eleanor explained. "We still are. Incommunicado, I mean."

"Mart worked the trick of getting us home." Paul was serious now. "He seemed to think you needed us more than the lieutenant, Penny."

Penny seized the head she had been pendulating from one to the other. "Perhaps I'm still out. Or maybe it's because I'm so glad to see you. And about Jay. But I can't make sense of what you say."

"Sit down, Paul. Eat your breakfast, Penny. I'll talk." Eleanor's voice was calm and firm. "It's a long story that

begins with last Tuesday night when I made the mistake
of asking Dr. Attilio to tell one of his diamond tales. And
he made the mistake of perpetrating that awful yarn about
Satan's Sixth Finger.

"That wasn't the first time he'd talked too much about
it. According to Lieutenant Diego, when he first received
the letter from the Bank of England, he was so excited he
told more than Paul and me. Mr. Cochrane— What's the
matter?"

"Nothing." Penny leaned back on her pillows and hid
her hands under the covers to conceal their trembling.
"Go on."

"Dr. Attilio told Mr. Cochrane and Wythe and perhaps
others. I can't criticize him, though, for I told Jay—"

"I know about Jay going to London to get the diamond."

"Thank heaven! I hated to confess what a fool I'd been.
Jay got the diamond to you, you to me, and I to Dr. Attilio—you know that too. And everything would have been
all right if he hadn't told that impossible tale—"

"I'll finish," Paul interrupted. "Interested Brazilian
officials learned of the stone too; I don't know how. But
because of the war there's a strict censorship now—perhaps through that. At any rate, someone at that stupid
dinner Tuesday night lost no time reporting that he suspected the stone had reached Dr. Attilio's hands. When we
tried to take a plane Wednesday morning he—this Diego
Machado—was right there to see we didn't.

"He had some fool idea we were taking Satan's Sixth
Finger back to New York to sell it. Anyway, he detained
us—very comfortably, I must admit—and as a reward for
our co-operation burned up the cables about Jay. That's
our story in a nutshell."

Paul lifted the breakfast tray from Penny's lap and
swung a chair round beside her. "Now I want to hear yours.

What's this about your destroying Madge Cochrane's happy home?"

"Paul! You don't know what you're saying!"

"I don't? Listen, my child. Eleanor and I used every persuasion and argument we could devise to induce Lieutenant Diego to permit us to return home. Nothing doing. Then yesterday Mart turns the trick by warning him of threats Madge was making against Cock and against you. And pronto! We were raced home after dark last night—to find you gone and Delfina with a fine tale about your goings on."

"Delfina!"

"Delfina says Madge has telephoned the Casa every day, demanding to speak to Cock. Refused to believe he wasn't here. It seems he has not been in his office most of this past week—"

"And he had been here," Eleanor interposed. "You told Madge that yourself, didn't you, Penny?"

Penny lifted a stricken face. "It's too late! Mr. Cochrane is dead. Madge killed him—yesterday afternoon!"

Paul and Eleanor sat motionless, incredulous.

"It's true!" she cried. "I saw him. And Madge—she was in Dr. Attilio's chapel—she tried to shoot Mart, I thought." Penny burst into hysterical laughter. "It wasn't Mart. It was I. I—I saved my own life!"

Paul leaned over and shook her hard. "Stop that, Penny. This can't be true! You're raving!"

"Let her alone, Paul," Eleanor took Penny's cold hands in hers, chafed them gently. "Whatever has happened isn't your fault, Penny. Madge has been very strange—these last two years. She was once such a lovely woman, so very much admired, but she's been ill, very ill."

"Ill!" Paul snorted. "She's been hag-ridden with jealousy! Of every woman Cock—" He strode about the room angrily. "But this can't be true, Eleanor. Penny's mistaken,

deluded. Mart would have told me. Where is he, anyway?"
He started for the door.

"You can't go out, remember, Paul. And you can't telephone," his wife warned. "Wait. It will do Penny good to
get everything off her mind. Listen to her first."

But Paul did not need to wait or listen. Delfina, her
eyes enormous with the news she bore, knocked and opened
the door.

"Mr. Paul, José says they're telling at the gatehouse
that Mr. Cochrane is dead. And Mr. Mart is coming up the
back hill—running." As she started to withdraw Delfina
added as an afterthought, "A man from the police is here
to see Miss Penny. His name is Diego Machado."

She disappeared, Paul on her heels.

But when Eleanor and Penny arrived in the living room
Dr. Attilio and Wythe were there also. Paul was busy pulling chairs into a semicircle about a cleared table near the
couch. On it Lieutenant Diego arranged papers from a fat
portfolio.

"Good!" he exclaimed as they entered. "Everyone is
here. I am sorry to confine you to a house on such a beautiful afternoon. With your aid, however, I may be able to
complete today our investigations into two complicated
situations that concern you all. Then you will be free."

He waited until everyone was seated, their attention
on him.

"Permit me first to clear away the minor difficulty that
concerns Fabrica da Luz alone. For more than two years, as
all but Miss Paget perhaps know, the Fabrica has suffered
increasingly heavy losses in lamps. The police were as unsuccessful as Mr. Oliver to discover the man or men steal-
ing them. Broken glass on the Fabrica walls, barbed wire,
added watchmen, and other precautions were of no avail.
Carton after carton left the Fabrica—until two months ago.

"By a coincidence the loss of lamps stopped with the departure of Mario Soares—the former superintendent of grounds—for New York. It was simple to assume, therefore, that his was the mind behind the thefts. But until last night we could not prove two things. How he had been able to get such quantities of lamps outside the walls. How, when he got them out, he was able to dispose of them.

"With Mr. Oliver's co-operation, we placed a man here as superintendent of grounds when Mario Soares left. Pedro Martins. 'Mart,' as you call him. He was unsuccessful, too, until he came upon the long-forgotten entrance to the old *subterraneo* that served this Casa Grande a century or more ago. The tunnel led to Dr. Attilio's home. Oddly Dr. Sloane and Miss Paget found that entrance yesterday also.

"If they had not gone through the *subterraneo* in the dark they would have come upon the small cell Mart found. Long ago it was used for disciplining insubordinate slaves. In that cell they might have seen an ingeniously concealed entrance to a branch tunnel that led straight to the workshop of a young Syrian cabinetmaker."

Eleanor and Dr. Attilio looked up, startled, then at one another. But the detective did not pause.

"A very skilled cabinetmaker. His work was in great demand, particularly in Juiz de Fora, the industrial city on the plateau behind the Organ Mountains. As you know, it connects by train and highway with many points in the interior. Trucks came weekly to his door to receive carefully boxed chests and desks and other pieces. To receive also, we know now, U. E. lamps to be sold as contraband."

Lieutenant Diego took up two photographs from the table. "One of these men is now in custody. One is dead. You will look at these photographs, please, and tell me if you recognize one or both of them." He gave them to Paul, sitting on his left.

"That's Mario Soares," Paul said to the first. "This fellow looks familiar, but I don't know him." He passed the photographs to Eleanor.

"Mario," she agreed. "And the other—it's Aladdin Barbuk! But you can't mean— Why, he's a wonderful little man. He made my desk out of an old Brazilian chest I found. I've sent him many customers." She started to pass the photographs across Penny to Dr. Attilio.

"You will look at them also, Miss Paget," the detective directed.

"But she can't know them," Eleanor protested. "Mario was gone long before she came, and Aladdin never left his shop."

"If you please, Miss Paget."

Penny took them with trembling fingers. She had already glimpsed the first photograph. At sight of the second she caught her breath.

"I—I know them both," she admitted slowly. "Though not by those names. This first one is Senhor Rodrigo who came down to Rio on the *Paraguay* with me. You know I know him, Lieutenant Diego. On the Avenida—"

The lieutenant said quickly, "And the other?"

Penny looked at Wythe, turned the photograph for him to see. "He—he said he was Hindu—a 'Mr. Mukerji.' He came here Thursday night to ask me to teach him English."

"He couldn't 'come here,' just like that!" Mart interjected. "You or Delfina had to telephone the gateman to admit him. I did my best with her, Paul," he added, "but she's impossible."

"You told me yourself it was all right to have people here," Penny retorted.

"Because I was under the impression you didn't know anyone to have!"

"Dr. Sloane, you will look at the photographs please." Lieutenant Diego's voice was peremptory, but his eyes amused.

Wythe took the pictures from Penny's hand. "Mario Soares. This one I don't know. I heard about Mukerji from Miss Paget but never saw him clearly enough to identify him." He offered the pictures to Dr. Attilio.

"Mario." Dr. Attilio turned from the first to the second quickly. "This is Aladdin, I regret to say. My wife will be desolate."

Mart took the photographs from him as he spoke and returned them to the detective. "I've already identified them for you, Lieutenant."

"Thank you. Since the entire contraband system rested on them you can now remove your broken glass and barbed wire, Mr. Oliver."

"With pleasure," Paul agreed. "But you only remove Mart over my dead body. Finder's keepers on Mart."

"Later I will learn that very concise phrase, Mr. Oliver. It seems to say much in little. But for the moment let us consider the matter of the missing lamps closed."

"One moment." Dr. Attilio put up a restraining hand. "You say that one man is dead, the other under arrest. May we know—"

Lieutenant Diego did not answer at once. He looked from face to face about him, then at the two photographs. In the silence suspense seemed to lie heavily on the air. The detective appeared to feel it, deliberately to prolong and exploit it. In sudden decision he tossed the pictures to the table, spoke briskly.

"Certainly, Dr. Attilio. The dead man is—Mario Soares."

Instantly his manner changed, became hard and direct. "The theft of the lamps is of importance here merely as a doorstep to murder. To the murder of Mario Soares—and of three other men. Their deaths must be added to the long list of victims credited to Satan's Sixth Finger."

20

Lieutenant Diego prolonged suspense by adding more papers from his portfolio to the collection on the table. Watching him, Penny understood in her own rising apprehension the sensations of the others. All continued to sit quietly in their chairs, but a tightening of the atmosphere in the room, the concentration of their eyes betrayed their inner tensity.

This was not lessened when at some gesture from the lieutenant two khaki-clad police entered from the kitchen, followed by Delfina. She seated herself on a straight chair some distance from the circle and became an image in whose face only two dark eyes moved. One of the policemen produced a notebook and sat down behind the circle also, pencil poised. The other stationed himself beside the fireplace.

By that time the atmosphere was electric. It practically crackled when Lieutenant Diego tipped a leather case from his portfolio. Opening it, he placed Satan's Sixth Finger on the table before them. In the shadow he threw over it it lay dull and inert, a rough and ugly thing and, perhaps because of the tradition linked with it, malignant.

The lieutenant's first words crackled too. "To save time I will sketch briefly my own part in this tragic story of the diamond."

Although he took up some typed sheets of paper he spoke without looking at them. "This is a copy of a letter received by Dr. Attilio de Sousa about a year ago from the Bank of England in London. From the time it came into my hands I naturally had an interest in Dr. Attilio's comings and goings. However, he made no change in his mode of life. It was only some weeks later when Mr. Jay Oliver applied for plane passport to Portugal, with visa to England and return, that we saw signs of a link between Dr. Attilio and his precious diamond.

"The applications were made through Mr. Emmett Cochrane, who explained he wished the young glassman to study new uses for glass under war conditions in England. We hastened to accommodate the president of so important an industry as the Universal Electric of Brazil.

"A month or so after Jay Oliver's departure Mario Soares applied for passport and plane passage to New York. His reason for going was simple and logical. He had saved sufficient money. Because of his connection with the Fabrica da Luz we made a record of his departure."

The detective turned to Dr. Attilio, sitting erect and stern in his chair. "You will confirm, will you not, Dr. Attilio, that Jay Oliver went to London in your behalf to secure the diamond?"

Dr. Attilio nodded his head gravely.

"And that in addition to various written credentials and authorizations, you gave him a letter to your kinsman, Dr. Rosario de Sousa, then in London, more or less as a refugee from Amsterdam?" When Dr. Attilio nodded again he asked, "Why?"

"Because it was necessary, senhor. As you must know, many proofs had to be provided the Bank of England before it could or would release so valuable a property. Dr. Rosario, as my kinsman, is also an heir to the diamond. He possesses, as I do, proof to his right in the form of a tiny key. Only these keys could unlock a small inner box contained in one or more larger ones. Either he or I had to be present in person with such a key."

Dr. Attilio moved to rise but, when the policeman stepped forward, sank back in his chair. "I was about to demonstrate what I am saying, Lieutenant," he explained with dignity.

Lieutenant Diego nodded. The policeman returned to his place. And Dr. Attilio, with an apologetic smile for Eleanor and Penelope, rose and removed his coat. Rolling back his left sleeve, he disclosed on his arm above the elbow a narrow circlet of gold. Penny's eyes widened as she saw hanging from it by a short gold chain a minute arm of gold and hand of silver.

Dr. Attilio removed the band and said directly to the detective, "In this little arm is a key to that inner box, similar to the one in Dr. Rosario's possession. You wish to see it?"

"If you please."

Dr. Attilio's hand closed over the little silver model. A swift movement and the silver hand separated from the gold arm. He moved forward to the table and tipped the arm. A liny key, hardly more than half an inch long, spilled out.

"Excellent." Lieutenant Diego's voice did not change, but his eyes showed sudden interest. "May I ask you to demonstrate again—with this?"

From an envelope before him he took out a duplicate gold arm and silver hand. Penny and Wythe leaned forward at sight of it, recognizing it by the fragment of broken chain in its top.

The detective spoke to Wythe. "Yes, I secured this and other things from your locked box this morning, Dr. Sloane. Later I will return the keys you lent me."

His face a study in conflicting emotions, Dr. Attilio continued to stand beside the table, looking at the second little arm on his hand. "May I ask where this was before it reached Dr. Sloane's private deposit box?" he asked coldly.

"In due time all will be explained, Dr. Attilio. You will open that, please?"

Without a word Dr. Attilio complied, laid arm, key, and hand on the table, and returned to his chair.

"Thank you," the detective said when he was seated. "You sent something else with Mr. Jay also?"

The ghost of a smile crossed the firm lips of the glass-factory director. "Some small rough pieces of glass."

"Good. That clarifies a confusing detail. I can now continue. Mr. Jay is a very intelligent young man. He mastered all the difficulties of traveling from Lisbon into war-torn England and found Dr. Rosario in London. Shortly they went together to the Bank of England and—unfortunately—after various interviews received Satan's Sixth Finger. I say unfortunately, for it would have been wiser to have allowed it to remain there—at least until Mr. Jay was ready to return to Rio. Dr. Rosario, as a diamond expert, however, wished to study the stone at length. Interest overcame judgment."

Unexpectedly the detective swung to another subject. "In London, also, was another member of the Sousa family. The English would call him a black sheep. This was Avila de Sousa, the younger brother of Dr. Rosario. Some years ago he left Brazil hastily."

"Twenty years ago," Dr. Attilio said coldly. "Under suspicion of having killed a brother officer."

"Thank you. Avila de Sousa, however, was a very able man. He had done very well for himself in London as an importer of South American products. It was in his home Mr. Jay found the old diamond expert.

"Senhor Avila became very curious about the arrival of a young American at such a time in London. More so when he was given no information that satisfied him. He made it his concern to know what absorbed his brother and the young American so deeply. He even followed or had them followed on their visits to the Bank of England.

"Becoming suspicious, Dr. Rosario, to test him, hid a piece or two of the glass, which after some difficulty Senhor Avila found. Whether he had some knowledge of Satan's Sixth Finger and the glass suggested it to him, or whether it merely whetted his interest, we do not know. We do know he determined to possess whatever it was Dr. Rosario had. He succeeded to the point of making it impossible for Mr. Jay and the stone to leave England together.

"Again Dr. Rosario and Jay Oliver used the glass pieces. They mailed them and Satan's Sixth Finger in identical boxes to various addresses. By ordinary registered mail! That is right, Dr. Attilio?"

"Yes. They mailed one to me. I knew when it arrived that Jay could not return to Rio, that he would go to New York and bring the stone down from there."

"Senhor Avila now put no obstacle in the way of Jay's departure. Nor Dr. Rosario's. In fact, he not only aided them to secure plane passages for New York from Lisbon, but accompanied them. And in New York Mario Soares—or Senhor Rodrigo, as Miss Paget knew him—quickly picked them up. How Mario knew they would arrive and when is a detail we have still to learn.

"Dr. Rosario, never a strong man, was now quite exhausted by strain and travel. Senhor Avila and Mario believed that if they could eliminate Jay—at least temporarily—they could deal with the old man. But first they had to locate the diamond. Jay, aware they were watching every step and word, made no effort to regain it.

"Shortly they relaxed their vigilance, first taking the rather stringent measure of half poisoning him. Unobserved, as he thought, he slipped away and called Miss Paget. Will you tell us what happened from then on, senhorita?"

As Penny described events in New York from the time she heard Jay's voice on the telephone until she sailed for Rio the faces about her were concerned and interested. All except Mart's.

"Never a dull moment," was his comment when she finished. "Do go on. I see now why you went into Rio alone, why you scoured the byways for Syrian cabinetmakers."

Wythe turned on him angrily, thought better of it, gave Penny an expressive glance and a cigarette.

"With your permission, Senhor Mart," Lieutenant Diego interrupted ironically, "I will add a few words, and then perhaps Miss Paget will go on. I wish only to say that with the aid of some New York acquaintances Mario undertook to secure the diamond and dispose of Jay. And, incidentally, of Avila. It was arranged that Avila should fly to Barbados and there wait for Mario and the diamond. Neither of them, of course, intended to return to Brazil. In fact, it was Mario's idea to secure the diamond for himself and cross the border into Canada."

The detective's penetrating black eyes traveling slowly about the room shone for an instant with satisfaction, but his smooth, clipped English never faltered.

"Mario did manage to dispose of Jay temporarily and locate the diamond. But he was unable to get it. Miss Paget had received it and concealed it in her hair. Though he bribed her nurse to secure it for him, the woman would not risk loss of her position, perhaps of her profession, to take it from Miss Paget by force. The diamond remained in Miss Paget's hair during her week in the hospital and throughout her voyage to Rio.

"Mario and Dr. Rosario also embarked with her on the *Paraguay*. Dr. Rosario naturally with reluctance. I understand he had Mario's word that if he sailed Jay would follow later. But again, although Mario was almost within reach of the. stone, he could not secure it. Dr. Rosario refused to permit him to approach Miss Paget, nor would he make any effort himself.

"As Barbados drew nearer Mario grew more desperate. For personal reasons—one of them that he must now be suspected of the lamp thefts at the Fabrica—he had no desire to return to Brazil. He believed all was lost, that he had no other recourse than to leave the ship at Barbados and go back to the United States. To retain his hold on Satan's Sixth Finger, however, he persuaded or forced the old man, sick and weak, to go ashore with him.

"But in Barbados was Avila de Sousa, a man of stronger will and cunning than his own. The result was that Mario and Avila returned to the *Paraguay*, leaving Dr. Rosario dead in an isolated spot on the island. Now if that is all clear—"

Wythe leaned forward. "Perhaps I shouldn't interrupt, Lieutenant Diego. But the nature of my work makes me wonder—"

"Ah yes! The scientific mind, Dr. Sloane. You feel I should state my authorities, prove all I have said. And you have reason. My authorities are Mr. and Mrs. Oliver, cables from Jay Oliver, what I learned from you and Dr. Attilio last night, and some sketchy, un-coordinated notes from Aladdin Barbuk. Because Mario Soares is not here to give me the details necessary, I am counting on the assistance of this group now."

"Of course." Wythe settled back. "Thank you, Lieutenant."

The detective turned to Penelope. "You will tell us what you heard and saw on the *Paraguay,* Miss Paget?"

Carefully and in detail Penny described the voyage. When she finished Eleanor turned on her reproachfully. "And you never told us, darling. No wonder you were exhausted."

"Listen to her!" Mart exclaimed. "I can hear her licking her chops from here. Don't let her deceive you, Dona Eleanor. Penny's made of India rubber."

"Senhor Mart!" Lieutenant Diego's voice was severe. "Miss Paget has contributed valuable information. We are all grateful to her. And there is much more to be said."

Silence fell quickly.

"I shall have to speak at this moment for Mrs. Cochrane," he continued. "And again my information is sketchy. She has told me her husband returned from the docks last Tuesday afternoon very much excited. For one thing, while watching the *Paraguay* berth, he recognized Mario Soares on an upper deck. He signaled to him and later, meeting him on the dock, accused him then and there of the Fabrica's losses. Mario first denied, then defied him to prove his charges. That made Mr. Cochrane very angry.

"At the same time, Mrs. Cochrane said, her husband seemed stirred over something else that had happened at the dock. He spoke of meeting Mrs. Oliver and Miss Paget there and was impatient to reach the Casa—to see Mr. Oliver."

Lieutenant Diego smiled oddly and paused to choose his words. "Mr. Cochrane, it seems, was an—ah—enthusiastic admirer of pretty young women. That may not surprise you who knew him. I confess, knowing him only by reputation as president of one of our leading industries in Brazil, it surprised me. But I—ah—have ample confirmation of his enthusiasm in reports I received this morning. Mrs. Cochrane, I believe, was not unaware of his—ah—tendencies and—"

"In other words, she was jealous," Paul interjected impatiently. "She was, very."

"Thank you. That is the word I wanted. When Mrs. Cochrane saw Miss Paget here at dinner last Tuesday night jealousy was the emotion she felt. She assumed Miss Paget to be the cause of her husband's interest in whatever happened at the docking of the *Paraguay*. I believe she made her—ah—feeling clear later." He looked at Eleanor questioningly.

"Delfina can tell you," Eleanor said reluctantly, "if it is necessary for you to know, Lieutenant."

"She called here every day," Delfina assured him, without invitation. "Sometimes many times a day. Once she came. And she said terrible things about Miss Penny."

"That is all we need to remember at the moment." With evident relief the detective turned to another subject.

"At the dinner here on Tuesday night you all heard Dr. Attilio tell the legend of Satan's Sixth Finger, with certain embellishments of his own to suggest if such a stone existed he did not have it. You all, including Mr. Cochrane, drew your own conclusions. And you were not too surprised the next day to learn that Mr. Oliver and his wife had taken the first plane for New York. Unaware that his son was the reason for his haste, you assumed—as I did—he was going with or because of the diamond.

"Our Internal Revenue Bureau naturally takes a deep interest in so valuable a stone. It was impossible to permit them to depart until the diamond had been properly appraised and taxed here. I detained them—comfortably, I hope."

"Lieutenant Diego!" Dr. Attilio was on his feet with indignation. "I must protest against any suggestion that I intended to defraud—"

"I was afraid you would, Dr. Attilio." The lieutenant looked properly regretful. "Of course we know your honorable and meticulous character. And Mr. Oliver's too, I must hasten to add. But after all, a million-dollar diamond could cause many honorable men to do strange things. And there was no time to investigate. We had to act. Let us make our peace later and turn again to Avila and Mario.

"Relations between them were becoming very strained. Each—and rightly—suspected the other of wishing to secure the stone for himself alone. Now I must return to the *Paraguay* for a moment to explain something Miss Paget did not know. Shortly after leaving Barbados, Mario, as Dr. Rosario's 'secretary,' received a charge slip and a copy of a wireless Dr. Rosario had sent to Dr. Attilio a few hours before. That wireless convinced him and Avila that the diamond had remained in New York. The reference to *Fouché*, they believed then, would tell where it could be found.

"Each determined to have the message for himself, discover the whereabouts of the stone, and leave the other to chew his nails. Separately they searched Miss Paget's cabin."

"But you said, Lieutenant," Mart pointed out, "Mario knew the stone was in Miss Paget's hair."

"Suspected is a better word. He did. But Avila, burned two or three times with those glass deceptions of Dr. Attilio's, believed that hair trick was a trick."

"The subtle Brazilian mind," Dr. Attilio murmured.

"Without message or diamond, they were desperate when the *Paraguay* docked," Lieutenant Diego went on, unheeding. "Then they met Mr. Cochrane. During the argument with Mario the U. E. *despachante,* Conçalves, came up, and Mr. Cochrane stopped talking to give him Miss Paget's keys and instructions about her luggage.

"Avila, a successful businessman himself and—ah—not unlike Mr. Cochrane in various ways, immediately saw in your U. E. president an opportunity and an ally. And Mr. Cochrane, for some reason of his own, after some discussion, became very receptive to Avila's persuasion.

They searched Miss Paget's luggage thoroughly, as she can doubtless testify."

"I can," Delfina announced. "I unpacked for Miss Penny."

The detective stepped round the table to face them.

"We come now to last Wednesday evening. The Olivers apparently are on their way to New York. Miss Paget is alone in this Casa. And Avila—possibly Mario, also—has learned from Mr. Cochrane that the Olivers are taking the diamond back with them. It is my impression—though I cannot prove it—that Mr. Cochrane thought in this way to avoid trouble."

"Mr. Cochrane told me something that might help you," Penny said unexpectedly. "He said he was trying to avoid a million-dollar-diamond scandal from involving the U.E. and Mr. Oliver and Dr. Attilio."

"So that's why he was so insistent on getting Mario behind bars!" Paul exclaimed. "The old fox! He never said a word about the diamond!"

"Avila and Mario merely became more frantic to secure the message about Fouché," the detective went on quickly. "For Wednesday evening, shortly after half-past nine, Avila entered the north gate of the Fabrica. With his military bearing and some sort of badge he managed to overwhelm the gateman and enter unannounced and unrecorded."

Lieutenant Diego threw out his slender hands dramatically. "Avila never returned to the north gate. Nor is he to be found in Rio. Last night. Dr. Sloane, you said you could give me proof of what happened to him."

Wythe hesitated. "Proof that a man was killed and his body destroyed on the Fabrica property, yes," he agreed slowly. "I cannot say it was Avila de Sousa."

"You forget. Miss Paget can."

As surprised glances turned on her Penny knew dismay. The presence of Avila's cane and tweeds in that little cell might not mean he was the murdered man after all. He had changed clothes with Dr. Rosario in Barbados. Perhaps he had again changed in that tunnel room.

Wythe's voice recalled her. "Penny, if you'll tell Lieutenant Diego what happened here from Wednesday night until you came to my office Thursday afternoon I'll carry on from there."

For the third time she was obliged to talk at length. Even Mart listened this time with the same concern and amazement as the rest. No one spoke when she finished. They simply looked at her until Wythe rose and, moving to the table, secured from Lieutenant Diego the two rough little chunks of glass and the Unprotecting Arm.

If they had listened to her with absorption they were even more spellbound by Wythe's clear explanations of his tests and deductions. Paul and Dr. Attilio, as glassmen, could not hear enough details. In spite of the detective's impatience to get on, they interrupted again and again with a heavy preponderance of questions. At last Wythe paused, took some papers from a pocket, turned to look at Penny.

"To state it simply, my first test proved that calcium and phosphorus had been added to the lead-glass mixture in Pot Seven of Number Two Furnace between five o'clock Wednesday afternoon and eight o'clock Thursday morning. My second test proved they existed in the surface of the mixture in almost the exact molecular ratio in which calcium and phosphorus exist in human bone. My third test proved that some small pieces of gold had also found their way into the mixture.

"Working last night and this morning—under somewhat difficult conditions—I completed the fourth and last test. To prove whether the gold in the glass mixture and the gold in the little arm Miss Paget found Thursday morning were the same or different My chemical analyses proved them to be identical."

"And that means—?" Lieutenant Diego prompted.

"That the body of the man Miss Paget saw on the steps of this Casa Wednesday night and the body of the man destroyed in Pot Seven later that same night were one and the same."

In the silence that followed Wythe laid the papers he was holding on the table beside the detective. "There is a complete report, including my analyses and deductions." He turned wearily and sank into his chair.

"It was Avila de Sousa," Dr. Attilio said heavily. "Only he could have taken the symbolic arm from Dr. Rosario's arm and placed it on his own. For Mario it would have had no significance."

"And your proof, Miss Paget?"

"I—I only know that the cane and gray tweeds this— Avila de Sousa wore on the *Paraguay* are lying in a little room off that tunnel."

Again that inexplicable sensation of fear seized her. In the pressure of the suddenly dead silence about her she could feel some threat, menace. She could not force her own eyes to lift to meet those she felt on her or force her lips to speak another word. Mart, on her left, released his breath slowly.

Dr. Attilio, motionless in his chair, became more immobile still, when the lieutenant stated rather than asked, "The deaths of Dr. Rosario de Sousa and Avila de Sousa leave you, Dr. Attilio, sole possessor of Satan's Sixth Finger."

21

Characteristically Lieutenant Diego swung to another topic. Picking up a flimsy from the table, he said briskly, "This is a copy of the wireless Dr. Rosario sent Dr. Attilio from the *Paraguay.*" He read it clearly, dropped it on the table again. "Avila, Mario Soares, and I all made various efforts to secure the biography of Fouché it refers to from Miss Paget. Yes, Dr. Sloane?"

"You have keen eyes, Lieutenant. I thought I was concealing my surprise rather well. It was you who had my apartment, my car, and myself searched on Sao João's Eve?"

"Your apartment and your car, yes, Doctor. Yourself, no. To my regret. If I had made a personal search of your apartment and your car that evening I would also have followed you and Miss Paget to the summit of Corcovado if necessary. In that case the loss of an important witness might have been averted."

Penny gasped. "Mario! Mario Soares was in the car that fell."

"He and Aladdin Barbuk followed you up the mountain. Only Aladdin came down," the detective finished for him.

"Accident?" Wythe asked.

"No. Blackmail. On Wednesday night Mario entered the Fabrica by way of Barbuk's shop and the *subterraneo,* to reach the Casa and secure the *Fouché*. As he reached the hedge, he saw Avila entering the Casa gates, followed him and, as you know, killed him on the Casa steps.

"Aladdin either followed Mario or, by other espionage of his own, knew of Avila's murder. He thought that isolated mountainside a good place and time to force Mario to give him a larger share in the diamond. Mario refused. Aladdin, driving, sent the car over the road and down, leaped clear himself."

With those horrible cries on Corcovado echoing in her ears, Penelope turned to Wythe. To her surprise he was leaning back, quite at ease. So, too, was Mart. In fact, Mart looked positively smug with satisfaction. And Dr. Attilio, sitting with lowered eyes, thoughtfully turning his ring round and round his finger, showed no regret for the former superintendent of grounds.

"Dr. Sloane," the lieutenant was saying, "I assume from the fact that Dr. Attilio, through you and Miss Paget, now has Dr. Rosario's message, that you know something about it. Will you tell us now?"

Concisely Wythe concentrated the long tale of his and Penny's adventures with the message from the finding of Fouché's biography Thursday night until the moment Penny placed it in Dr. Attilio's hands. "I did not make a copy of it," he concluded. "And I see no reason for such a message nor all the trouble it has caused. It consists merely of measurements and recommendations about the stone."

"You also have read the message, Dr. Attilio?"

Dr. Attilio nodded. "Dr. Sloane is quite right. The message he read contains nothing more. I may say he had hidden it so ingeniously that it required more time to find than to read."

"Later I will ask for the book and a copy of the message. But the afternoon is coming to an end, and we have one more death to account for. Mr. Emmett Cochrane's."

Another, deeper silence fell over the room. The policeman, at a signal from Lieutenant Diego, went out by way
of the foyer. They listened to his footsteps on the polished
floor of the reception *sala*. A moment later listened to
them returning, muffled by others.

Eleanor started as the stately figure of Dona Margherita appeared in the foyer archway. Her arm supported the
small, shrinking form of Madge Cochrane. Behind them
walked the policeman.

Everyone sprang up. But Lieutenant Diego motioned
them back to their seats. Mart was placing chairs for Dona
Margherita and Mrs. Cochrane beside the lieutenant's
table.

Madge sat down quickly, her white, drawn face bent
forward, her hands gripped tight on a handkerchief she
had twisted into a rope. Dona Margherita stood a moment, her dark eyes sparkling with anger as she looked
about the circle. They rested on her husband before, with
slow dignity, she seated herself beside Mrs. Cochrane.

Lieutenant Diego's voice was grave, sympathetic. "I
understand how painful this hour must be—for all of
you. We will be as brief as possible. Sunday afternoon Mr.
Cochrane was killed by a shot from his own revolver. The
nature of the wound precludes any possibility of suicide.
Sunday evening—late—I found Mrs. Cochrane, the revolver still in her hand, in the chapel of Dr. Attilio. She
denies, however, either the intention or the act."

His voice lost its note of understanding. "Senhores and
senhoras, I only want the truth. I believe I can find it
among you. Let us be as frank and explicit as we can. Dr.
Sloane, I believe you were the last person to see Mr. Cochrane alive, were you not?"

"Until I know the time of his death I cannot answer
that question with any certainty. I saw him, talked with

him for a few minutes early Sunday afternoon. About half-past two, I think. In my office."

"By appointment?"

"Decidedly by accident. After all that had happened Saturday, particularly climbing Corcovado with Miss Paget, I could neither sleep nor rest on Sunday. Finally, after luncheon, I came out to my laboratories. I thought I might as well finish work on that fourth test. That is, after I had telephoned the Casa and learned from Delfina that Miss Paget was still sleeping."

He turned to Delfina. "Do you remember what time I called?"

"A little more than two hours," she answered promptly.

"It was considerably after that when I hung up the receiver. Delfina went into details about what she thought of that climb. Just as I hung up Mr. Cochrane appeared in my office doors."

Wythe's tone changed. "I was both surprised to see him and to see that he was very much upset about something. He had come out to talk with Mart about Mario being in Rio, he said. When he could not find Mart he stopped in to ask if I had seen him. I had not, and after a few minutes he left. I worked in the laboratories for an hour or more, then locked up and went home. I had only been there a few minutes when Delfina phoned for me to come to the laboratories as quickly as possible. I took a taxi—I'd used buses for my earlier trip—and was back here before six."

"Did you mention this to Miss Paget or anyone?"

"That I'd seen Mr. Cochrane? No, I don't think so. It was just a chance meeting—no reason to remember or mention it."

"Sloane's right about times," Mart corroborated unexpectedly. "The gate records show he came in at two-five, left at three-thirty, returned at five-fifty-five. Mr. Cochrane checked through the north gate at two-eighteen. Mrs. Cochrane at three-fifteen."

Lieutenant Diego looked at Mrs. Cochrane. "Will you repeat what you told me last night, senhora? Or would you prefer to answer questions?"

"Questions," Mrs. Cochrane murmured without looking up.

"Good. Why did you come to Fabrica da Luz on Sunday afternoon?"

"My husband said he was coming here to see Wythe Sloane and Mart. I did not believe him. I thought—"

"He was coming to see Miss Paget?" the detective completed when her voice faltered.

She nodded slightly. "He—I thought he—came to see her every day. I wanted—to be sure—"

"And when you were sure what did you intend to do?"

"I didn't mind—so much—his interest in—in entertainers and others. But I couldn't bear it to be Eleanor's—Mrs. Oliver's friend."

Madge Cochrane lifted her head, flung the handkerchief from her. "I was jealous, frantic with jealousy. I thought if he were interested in someone like Miss Paget—I had really lost him. I wanted to be sure. If it were true I had decided to—to return to the States. To divorce him."

"You did not bring his revolver with you?"

"Of course not. He brought it himself. At least he always had it—in the pocket of his car."

"And you believe he had an appointment with Dr. Sloane?"

"He didn't say so. But he seemed to know Wythe would be at his laboratories."

"Perhaps he called my apartment, asked my maid," Wythe suggested.

"And when you entered the north gate what did you do, senhora?"

"I came out by a taxi but dismissed it at the gate." Madge Cochrane's voice was low but steadier now. "I walked from the north gate on the pavement past the laboratories and warehouses and came up the back hill road to the rear Casa gates. The front driveway is too steep for me and—I didn't want to be seen—at first. Near the rear gates I met Delfina, and she convinced me my husband was not in the Casa. She said that except for a few minutes one morning he had never been there."

"And then?" prompted Lieutenant Diego.

"I started back the way I had come. But I was awfully tired. And I dreaded returning to Rio alone. I thought perhaps I could find my husband and looked around for his car. From the back road I could see it parked between a warehouse and the laboratories. I started down the hill toward it. Then I saw Mart—"

She stopped uneasily. "He was running. Toward his shops. And something about him or the way he was running frightened me. My husband had come out to see him and—they didn't get on together very well—"

"And then?"

"I ran, too. To the warehouse where the car was. I tried all the doors and pounded on them, but I could hear nothing. I didn't know what to do. The laboratory doors had been closed when I passed, but I went there anyway. They were still closed, but when I pounded on them one opened. A little."

Tears began to roll down Madge Cochrane's cheeks. She seemed unaware of them and continued to look at the lieutenant. With a gesture he stopped Dona Margherita's attempt to give her a handkerchief.

"I pushed it a little more. And saw my husband. Lying on the floor. Not in the office. Just inside the laboratories. I—I went in. He was dead. And that revolver was near his hand. But I don't remember picking it up. I don't remember anything except standing there with everything broken and heaped around."

"You have been very good to tell this so clearly, Mrs. Cochrane. Rest now for a time. Mart will tell us why he was running, why he found you in the laboratories."

Mart spoke immediately and with something of the clipped restraint of the lieutenant. "I was running because I was mad. Mr. Cochrane promised, by one o'clock, to be at the north gate. And after hours of waiting for him I find his car beside the warehouse! 'He's gone to my office,' I think—as if I'd wait there for him until almost four o'clock.

"I ran over but he wasn't there. So I smoked a cigarette to cool down. Then I started back for the gatehouse to leave a message for him that I wasn't playing any more. As I passed the laboratories I saw one of the doors open. 'He might be there,' I think. Doc Sloane often works Sundays and evenings. What I find is the place a shambles and in the midst of it Mrs. Cochrane standing over her husband, a gun in her hand. She acted like a frozen woman. Couldn't move, couldn't speak. I got her out, locked up with my own keys, and took her to Dona Margherita. *Mamãe* wasn't home."

He looked at Dr. Attilio as if for confirmation and rushed on. "It was almost four-thirty then. It is almost five when I arrive back at the laboratories—just in time to see Miss Paget racing up the hill, screaming for Delfina. 'She couldn't have been in the laboratories,' I think, 'but she must have discovered something.' And I didn't want that body found on the premises. (I'm already a U.E. man enough not to want scandal to touch the place.) And I didn't dare move it far. Then I remembered the discovery I made Saturday afternoon."

Mart grinned sardonically. "My discovery was the reason why Mr. Cochrane condescended to join my humble self. Saturday morning I'd burned over the dry grass above the laboratories. Late that afternoon, kicking over the

ground to see that my men had done a good job, I came on
that *tanque* full of junk. 'Mario,' I say to myself, 'was the
kind of superintendent to let that stuff stay there forever.'
But not me! I started to heave it out and discovered it to
be the neatest bit of camouflage of all time. It concealed
a trap door.

"I explored the *subterraneo* beneath it as far as a stone-
walled cell. There's a false door there and behind that door
a passage that actually contained some U.E. cartons. That
passage was short and led to Barbuk's shop. Mr. Cochrane
had been pressing me for proof against Mario. Here it was!
I made a date with him by phone to meet me in the Fabrica at one o'clock on Sunday. We thought no one would be
here and we could explore—"

"Yes, yes," Lieutenant Diego interrupted impatiently,
"but the point is—"

"The point is that the *tanque* entrance is just a few
steps from the laboratories. I carried Mr. Cochrane's body
to that cell."

"That is all you have to say?"

"Unless you'd be interested to know I was just coming out of the *subterraneo* again—about six o'clock—when
Dr. Sloane came running through the north gate and Miss
Paget down the hill. I ducked back until they went into
the laboratories."

"And then?"

Mart shifted position uncomfortably.

"Well, then I sort of stood by—to see what they'd do.
They remained inside for hours. When they came out they
went straight to the *tanque*—as if they'd always known
about it—"

"You followed us," Penny accused coldly.

"For a time, yes. But you remained so long in that
cell I thought you'd found the concealed door and gone
into the branch tunnel. I'd promised Dr. Attilio to return

as soon as I could to decide what to do next about Mrs. Cochrane. So I left the *subterraneo,* drove over to his home. I was talking with him and Mrs. Cochrane when you began to hammer on that door. I left before he admitted you and returned—"

"We'll leave you for a moment," the detective interrupted, "and turn to Dr. Sloane and Miss Paget. Their story should fit in here."

22

For the next half-hour Lieutenant Diego led Penny and Wythe back and forth over their experiences in the laboratories, their discovery of the *subterraneo,* their arrival in Dr. Attilio's library. Again and again he harped back to one question. Why had they concealed from Dr. Attilio that they had stopped in the little cell, seen Mr. Cochrane's body there?

"Oh, make your own interpretation," Wythe finally said wearily.

"You've said you didn't suspect Dr. Attilio, Wythe," Paul pointed out. "If you think Mart killed Mr. Cochrane, was spying on you, say so. Mart can defend himself later. If it's Penny you're trying to shield, forget it. Lieutenant Diego's being as considerate as he can. The least we can do is to tell him anything we know or even suspect."

Wythe admitted reluctantly, "I couldn't forget then—in the tunnel—that it was Penny who discovered Mr. Cochrane's body in my laboratories. That it was Penny who led me straight to the *tanque,* who insisted we explore the *subterraneo* though it was late and about to rain. Penny who found that cell and Cochrane's body. Perhaps it was the sight of my ruined laboratories, perhaps the accumulation of everything that had happened which got me down. I couldn't be sure she hadn't led me there deliberately."

"Wythe!" Penny turned on him incredulously.

He smiled wryly. "If Paul wants the whole truth I even suspected when I heard someone in the passage behind us that you had led me into a trap."

"A trap! You? How could I?"

"Why not?" Mart's voice was harsh with impatience. "He's in a trap now. And knows it!"

Wythe leaped to his feet. Mart tilted back in his chair, his lips stretched in a provoking grin, but his eyes alert.

"Sit down, please, Dr. Sloane," Lieutenant Diego said quietly.

"I shall not sit down, Lieutenant. I've had enough." Wythe took an angry stride toward the doors. The policeman was there before him.

"What is this? I've told you all I know!"

"Not quite all, Dr. Sloane. I had hoped to carry this outline of events to a conclusion. But Mart's impatience anticipated me."

"What do you mean, Lieutenant?"

"That you haven't told us why you sent Mario Soares to New York. How Mario knew Jay Oliver and Dr. Rosario would arrive there. Why Mario knew to sail on the *Paraguay* with Miss Paget."

"How can I answer such fantastic questions?"

"Suppose I tell you we know you learned her son's plans from Mrs. Oliver. That you knew of the close friendship between the Olivers and Miss Paget. That when the cable arrived announcing her coming to Rio, you suspected she was bringing Satan's Sixth Finger and cabled Mario.

"You began to suspect Mario of trickery, didn't you, when he didn't report to you on his return to Rio? And when your own experiments proved Miss Paget's belief that a man had been killed and his body destroyed in the glass factory, you suspected Mario as the murderer, didn't you?"

"Interesting. Very. And whom did I think he killed, Lieutenant Diego? I knew Mario as Mr. Oliver, Dr. Attilio, everyone knew him, merely as the superintendent of grounds."

"You also knew him as the man responsible for the lamp thefts, didn't you? Wasn't that knowledge the whip you held over him to force him to do your bidding? The only thing you did not know was his way of getting the lamps outside the walls. But you believed if he knew a secret way out he also knew a way in!"

"Suppose I tell you, Dr. Sloane," the detective was continuing, "that your excellent work in making the analyses and deductions about the death of the man we know now to have been Avila de Sousa, and in discovering, deciphering, and guarding the message from Dr. Rosario was not the work of a disinterested friend either of Miss Paget or justice. It was a skillful and determined effort to be prepared to protect yourself."

When Wythe remained silent the detective added slowly, "Suppose I tell you the message you guarded so effectively was not the real message—that it merely served to conceal another. Only darkness was necessary to reveal the first. But darkness plus heat had to be applied to uncover the real warning Dr. Rosario sent his kinsman."

"I would remind you that I am a chemist, Lieutenant." Wythe smiled then. "Such a thing is impossible."

"Dr. Rosario was also a chemist. Dr. Attilio is a chemist. Listen. Here is the real message."

The detective slipped a sheet of paper from the bottom of a pile and read:

With misgivings I send this to warn you of a Mario Soares whom you know. Avila followed

us to New York. M. S. was there. They joined
to keep us under constant surveillance. Jay has
disappeared. So, too, has Avila. I fear for my
own life and have agreed to debark at Barbados
and return to New York. Guard yourself against
M. S. if the stone reaches you safely. Even more
against a man more dangerous still whom M. S.
fears and will betray if he can. I do not know
this man's name, but he is close to Jay's family,
for he learns and anticipates our every move.
From New York I will write you fully.

As the detective finished reading Wythe leaned forward to crush out his cigarette, leaned back.

"You are a very clever man, Dr. Sloane. You see at once that the message does not mention your name. And you have covered every action well under guise of assisting or protecting Miss Paget. Yet it is true, is it not, Mrs. Oliver, that you repeated to Dr. Sloane news you received from your son?"

Eleanor nodded slowly.

"And to no one else?"

She shook her head.

"You forget, perhaps, Lieutenant," Wythe pointed out, "your own excellent censorship—"

"I forget nothing, Doctor, not even a detail that Mrs. Cochrane mentioned last night but neglected to repeat today. That shot from her husband's gun in Dr. Attilio's library was intended for you, senhor. Watching you through the chapel gates, Mrs. Cochrane remembered the quarrel between you and her husband last Saturday afternoon when he refused to accept your resignation until Mr. Oliver returned. She remembered her husband's suspicion late Saturday when Mart called to say he had found Mario's secret exit so near your laboratories."

"Mr. Cochrane's sense of suspicion was well developed, I admit, Lieutenant Diego," Eleanor broke in, "but that seems very farfetched to me."

"Not when you consider the relation of warehouse to laboratories and laboratories to *subterraneo*, senhora. It would have been difficult to remove large lamp cartons from warehouse to *subterraneo* directly. They either had to be carried in front of the laboratories or back of them. A method dangerous indeed, considering that watchmen ranged the grounds at all hours. But to carry the cartons across the passage between warehouse and laboratories and through them to the *tanque* was very simple. At night the *tanque,* high above the heads of anyone on the pavement, cannot be seen, and that section of hillside was never patrolled, I believe."

Wythe laughed shortly. "Are you accusing me of petty thievery now?"

"Not at all. I suggest that when you discovered Mario to be using your laboratories for his thefts you threatened exposure unless he did as you asked. You thought him too dumb—as he was—to dare to steal the diamond for himself. But I see your purpose. You are diverting me from Mrs. Cochrane's attempted vengeance."

"Vengeance! Madge Cochrane?"

Mrs. Cochrane looked up, rose uncertainly. "I did try to kill you, Wythe. You deserved it. I can't prove it, but I'm sure you killed my husband when he accused you—"

Wythe turned to Paul. "Can you sit there and hear these charges without a word? You know me and my work."

Paul looked back at him steadily. "If you are innocent you can prove it, Wythe. If you are guilty Lieutenant Diego must prove it."

"How can I prove it?" Wythe demanded. "Mario Soares is dead. Mr. Cochrane is dead. And this Dr. Rosario. They condemn me with dead men's words."

"One moment, Dr. Sloane. I hoped to permit you to convict yourself with your own words. I think you have. Why, as Miss Paget asked, should you suspect a trap if you are innocent? However, I can produce a living man."

The policeman was already hurrying toward the veranda doors. Shortly he reappeared on the veranda followed by three men. Two wore khaki uniforms. The third, slender and dapper in civilian dress, walked between them. They marched into the living room to stop inside the doors.

"Mario Soares did not die on Corcovado, Dr. Sloane. Aladdin Barbuk was the man who went over the precipice in a car."

Wythe started up, took a step forward. Then as a slow, evil smile moved on Mario's red lips, in his black eyes, he stopped short. For a moment Wythe looked about the room, reading in each face understanding of that smile.

With a shrug he turned and silently walked to the table. Unrestrained by the detective, he took up Satan's Sixth Finger. No one stirred as he turned it slowly in his own long fingers, closed his hands over it for an instant.

"To make sure its tradition does not fail me," he said coolly. "I have no desire to live longer—a poor man."

He placed the diamond on the table and looked at the detective. "Because of that smirking fool whom you led me to believe dead, I am caught—trapped. And at your disposal, Lieutenant. It is true I wanted the diamond. It is true I killed Mr. Cochrane when he accused me of aiding Mario in the lamp thefts and to steal the stone. But I killed him in self-defense. He tried to force a confession from me with his gun. I took it from him, shot him. I knew the diamond had escaped me, that two men had died because of it. But with Mr. Cochrane and Mario dead, I thought myself clear."

Paul was on his feet, staring at Wythe. "But, Wythe, whoever killed Cock destroyed your laboratories. You couldn't—wouldn't—" He stopped short.

Wythe's cool, controlled face was draining slowly white. Suddenly it suffused with rage, and he swung round on the detective.

"You didn't know!" he shouted. "You didn't really know! I destroyed my laboratories because I thought no one would believe I'd do that. And no one did believe it! You couldn't have proved—"

"No," Lieutenant Diego told him evenly. "We couldn't have proved you killed Mr. Cochrane. Even Mario could have proved you guilty only of an attempt to steal the diamond. If you had not touched Satan's Sixth Finger, Dr. Sloane, we might still believe Mrs. Cochrane killed her husband. You lost your head, senhor, when you took that stone in your hands."

He motioned to the policemen. Wythe saw the gesture, went to meet them. Without a backward glance he strode ahead of them through the doors.

In silence, incredulous, stricken, those left behind remained seated, looking after him. Lieutenant Diego quietly replaced his papers, the chunks of glass and other objects in his portfolio. He left the diamond until the last. For a moment he looked at it somberly, as if reluctant himself to touch it. Then he swept it swiftly into its case and into the portfolio.

With a bow he turned for the doors. Paul rose and went with him.

The others rose, too, to leave. Only Penny remained in her chair. Mart, not far away, stood watching her, his eyes neither derisive nor sardonic now.

After a time he moved to her side, placed a hand on her shoulder. "Don't take this too hard," he said gently. "Doc Attilio would say this was another case of Americans wanting more than they have. Sometimes they get it. Sometimes—they don't."

"You knew—all the time?"

"Suspected. No one knew."

Penny turned from him. "Oh, go away. I never want to see you again!"

"Don't say that, Penny. Please. I won't play American any more. And I'm rather nice as a Brazilian. Now this is over, I'll show you Rio. One beautiful day, all Brazil. Make you forget—"

"One day? You mean you, too, want—?"

"More than I have? No. I want you, my *Pennyzinha*. Now I have the chance to make you want me. You don't now. But you will. One beautiful day—"

About the Author

Vera Kelsey (1892-1961) was the daughter of an American couple, born in Winnipeg, Ontario. She grew up in Grand Forks, North Dakota. She was a reporter for the *Fargo Forum,* and graduated from the University of North Dakota. Her early writing career included working for the *North China Daily News,* which allowed her to travel extensively in Asia, and then she spent almost five years in South America, particularly Brazil, before making her home in New York. She wrote mystery novels, travel books, and historical and regional nonfiction. She spent her last years in Minneapolis, and owned a cottage on Lake Minnetonka.

THE OWL
SANG
THREE
TIMES

VERA KELSEY

Coachwhip
Publications

THE BRIDE
DINED
ALONE

VERA KELSEY

CoachwhipBooks.com

**Coachwhip
Publications**

WHISPER
MURDER!

VERA KELSEY

FEAR
CAME
FIRST

VERA KELSEY

CoachwhipBooks.com

FULL CRASH DIVE

ALLAN R. BOSWORTH

Coachwhip
Publications

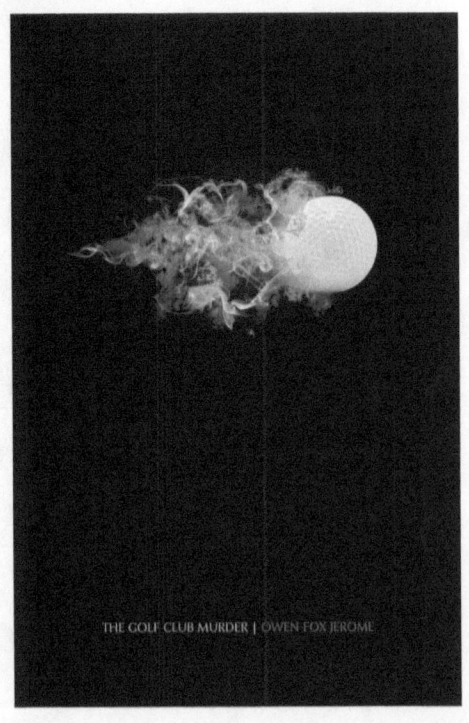

THE GOLF CLUB MURDER | OWEN FOX JEROME

CoachwhipBooks.com

Coachwhip
Publications

CoachwhipBooks.com

Death at **Windward Hill**

Murder in the **French Room**

HELEN JOAN HULTMAN

Coachwhip Publications

THE HEX MURDER

Alexander Williams

CoachwhipBooks.com

Coachwhip Publications

Hugger Mugger in the Louvre
Elliot Paul

No Face to Murder
EDITH HOWIE

CoachwhipBooks.com

**Coachwhip
Publications**

THE SERGEANT HARTY MYSTERIES
JOEL Y. DANE

MURDER CUM LAUDE
①
THE CABANA MURDERS

LAVERNE RICE
WELL DRESSED
FOR MURDER

Coachwhip
Publications

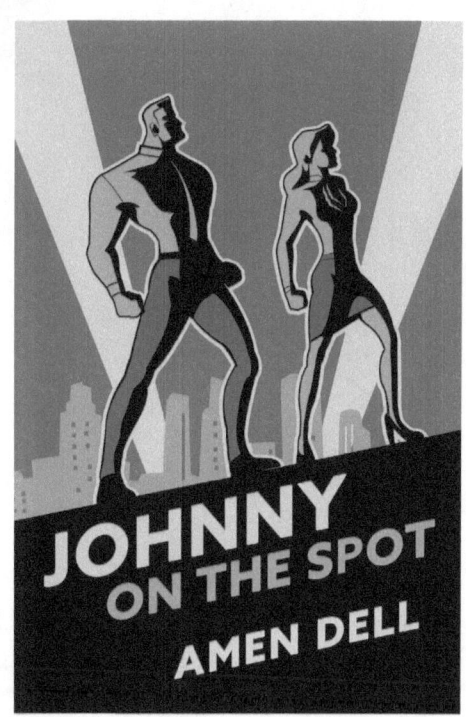

CoachwhipBooks.com

Coachwhip
Publications

CoachwhipBooks.com

www.ingramcontent.com/pod-product-compliance
Lightning Source LLC
Chambersburg PA
CBHW050416260626
47156CB00003B/1033